"I'd like to get to k

His eyes turned serious
about if we start fresh, p
we do that tonight?"

She tried to speak but could get nothing past her throat, not even breath.

You can't pretend that, her conscience protested. *Tell him about his son. He needs to know.*

"Nate," she finally managed. "I think it would be best if—"

He touched her lips. "Think less. This one time."

He pulled her chair closer, close enough for him to cup the back of her head. "On second thought, you should know my intentions before we set our plans in stone." His voice was so soft.

Her heart beat so hard she could barely draw the breath to speak. "What are your intentions?"

Tenderly his lips settled on hers, soft as down. How could she have forgotten the feel of them, the scent of his skin? It was a homecoming.

She kissed him back with yearning and passion and a hunger she couldn't satisfy on a neighborhood porch.

This is wrong, her conscience cried out.

If it was, it was an exquisite, magnificent mistake.

THE MEN OF THUNDER RIDGE:
Once you meet the men of this Oregon town,
you may never want to leave!

Dear Reader,

In a valley below a snowcapped mountain called Thunder Ridge lies a small Oregon community with wooden sidewalks, a winding river and one down-on-her-luck waitress who, a long time ago, fell in love with local golden boy Nate Thayer.

Theirs was a true Cinderella story...only without the happy ending. Until, fifteen years later, fate gave them a second chance...

I loved creating the town of Thunder Ridge and the people who live there. They're strong and passionate, funny and, ultimately, I think, very brave. Love requires courage, doesn't it? Sometimes we have to overcome our fears and hesitations and dive in. Izzy and Nate's relationship is like that. It's going to take all the courage they can muster to overcome past mistakes, big secrets and hurt hearts. But they can do it. We all can.

I hope you enjoy Izzy and Nate's story, the first book in my new miniseries, The Men of Thunder Ridge. And don't forget: every day you're writing the most important story of all—your own!

With love,

Wendy

His Surprise Son

———

Wendy Warren

HARLEQUIN®SPECIAL EDITION®

Recycling programs
for this product may
not exist in your area.

ISBN-13: 978-0-373-65972-2

His Surprise Son

Copyright © 2016 by Wendy Warren

Printed in U.S.A.

Wendy Warren loves to write about ordinary people who find extraordinary love. Laughter, family and close-knit communities figure prominently, too. Her books have won two Romance Writers of America RITA® Awards and have been nominated for numerous others. She lives in the Pacific Northwest with human and non-human critters who don't read nearly as much as she'd like, but they sure do make her laugh and feel loved.

Books by Wendy Warren

Harlequin Special Edition

Once More, At Midnight
Undercover Nanny
Making Babies
Dakota Bride

Home Sweet Honeyford

Caleb's Bride
Something Unexpected
The Cowboy's Convenient Bride

Logan's Legacy Revisited

The Baby Bargain

Family Business

The Boss and Miss Baxter

Silhouette Romance

The Oldest Virgin in Oakdale
The Drifter's Gift
Just Say I Do
Her Very Own Husband
Oh, Baby!
Romantics Anonymous
Mr. Wright

Visit the Author Profile page
at Harlequin.com for more titles.

For my daughters, Liberty and Elliana, beautiful
through and through. Thank you for being
my teachers, my miracles, and for having
the best laughs in the world. I love you.

Chapter One

Thunder Ridge, Oregon

Izzy Lambert considered herself an honest person, and she'd bet her last dollar that most people who knew her would agree. In her whole life, she'd told only two whoppers. And if you wanted to get technical about it, the first was really more a lie of omission than an outright fib.

She'd spent a whole lot of time afraid her secrets would be discovered and nearly a decade and a half on the lookout for the man from whom she'd withheld the truth. Sometimes she'd think she was seeing him…

…at the Thunderbird Market, reaching for a quart of creamer in the dairy aisle…

…in line at the bank…

…in the car behind hers at the Macho Taco drive-through in Bend…

And once she'd nearly choked on a Mickey Mouse

pancake at Disneyland, because she thought he was there, pushing a double stroller.

In reality, it never had been him—*thank you, God*— but each time Izzy thought she saw Nate Thayer, her heart began to pound, her pulse would race, she'd feel hot and dizzy, and flop sweat drenched her in seconds.

Kinda like right now.

"Join us for lunch at The Pickle Jar. A joke and a pickle for only a nickel," she said distractedly as she handed a flyer to a group of tourists. Her eyes darted from their sun-burned faces to the tall, dark-haired man at the far end of the opposite side of the block.

One of the women waggled the flyer. "Is this a genuine New York deli?"

"It's a genuine Oregon deli," Izzy murmured, squinting into the distance. She remembered a headful of thick black hair just like on the man down the block. And broad, proud shoulders like his.

"Where is it?" one of the other women asked.

"About a hundred feet that way." Taking several mincing steps, Izzy made a half turn and pointed. As she turned back, a tour bus pulled up, blocking the man from her view. *Dang it!*

"Is that why you're dressed like a pickle?" asked an elderly gentleman who was perspiring in the sun almost as much as she was.

Admonishing herself to concentrate on the prospective customers, she forced a smile. "I'm not just any pickle— I'm a kosher dill."

Yeah, she was dressed in a foam rubber pickle suit, the latest in her series of desperate attempts to scare up some new customers for the aged deli. "The Pickle Jar has quarter-done, half-done and full dill pickles, all homemade from a secret family recipe. You can take some home in a collector jar, too."

According to her online class, Branding is Your Business, having a mascot emphasized the idea behind the product, built connections with customers and humanized the company. Although one could argue that a pickle was not human.

It wasn't as if she *enjoyed* dressing as a giant briny cucumber. Once upon a time Izzy had imagined herself in college, studying business, then having an office of her own and wearing beautiful professional attire. Of course, once upon a time she'd imagined a lot of things that had turned out to be nothing more than fantasies. She'd learned several years back that you couldn't move forward unless you were first willing to accept reality. So with The Pickle Jar losing potential customers every day to the newer, hipper eateries in town, Izzy had succumbed to desperate measures, even going online to purchase this warty green pickle suit, only "slightly" used.

It was swelteringly hot and dark inside the costume, and the cylindrical interior could use a good steam cleaning. None of the other deli employees would even consider putting it on. But she did, because the costume was a marketing tool and allowing the business to close was not an option.

The tourist to whom she'd been speaking, dressed in the same Keep Portland Weird T-shirt as his wife, crossed his arms. "Can we really get a joke and a pickle for just a nickel?"

"Absolutely."

She spared one last glance across the street, but the tour bus was still in the way. With perspiration trickling below the wimple-style head of the pickle suit, she swiped her brow. The man she'd thought she recognized was probably gone, anyway. Believing she saw Nate Thayer was nothing more than a weird function of her overanxious mind. For some reason, it was almost always in times of personal stress that she would imagine she saw him. Probably because she could think of few things *more* stressful than having to confront him again.

Focus on business, she counseled herself. *Business is real.*

The Pickle Jar wasn't only her place of employment; it was her home. It was where she'd discovered family for the first time in her life. She was the manager of a failing restaurant, but she could fix it. She *would* fix it.

Forgetting about everything else, Izzy returned her focus to the tourists and gave them her most gracious smile. "I've got a million jokes, but the pickles are even better. Follow me to the best little deli west of the Hudson."

So far, Nate Thayer's trip down memory lane was proving bumpier than anticipated. Seated across from Jackson Fleming, who'd quarterbacked for Ridge High back in the day, Nate listened with half an ear as his former teammate complained about…ah, pretty much everything, from the boredom of driving a milk truck for a living to the pressures of raising four kids who sucked up every penny he made, to the slowness of the service at The Pickle Jar, where, in fact, they hadn't been seated for more than a couple of minutes and were currently perusing the plastic-coated menus.

In Thunder Ridge on business, this was Nate's first trip home in fifteen years. It had been his suggestion to have lunch here, and while Jack griped about life post high school, Nate allowed his attention to wander around the deli. On the surface, not much had changed. He remembered sitting at that chipped Formica counter, studying for his final high school exams, nursing a drink and eating his fill of mouth-puckering pickles until Sam Bernstein started sending over free corned beef on rye. "Eat," the older man, short of stature but huge of heart, had insisted when Nate refused the gratis meals at first. "I see you in here all the time, studying hard." Sam had nodded his approval. "The brain needs food. I'm making a contribution to your college education. You'll thank me by having a good career."

He did have a good career, a great career actually, as a commercial architect based in Chicago. Over the years, when he'd thought of Thunder Ridge, he'd found himself hoping the Bernstein brothers would approve. Today Nate didn't see either of the two old men who owned the deli. The force of his desire to find them alive and well surprised him. He had written once or twice after he'd left for college, but there'd been a lot of water under the bridge, too many complicated feelings for the communication not to feel awkward; soon it had fallen away altogether. Nate wouldn't be in town long, but it would feel good to mend that particular fence.

His relationship with the brothers was not the only casualty from his past, of course, but the other issue was unlikely to ever be repaired. Isabelle Lambert had left town shortly after he had. In high school, he and Izzy had been in different grades and had run with different crowds; he hadn't so much as heard her name in a decade and a half. More than once he'd thought about looking her up but had always talked himself out of it.

Nevertheless, it was impossible to return to Central Oregon and not think about the girl with the caramel hair, skin soft as a pillow and lake-colored eyes so big and deep Nate had wanted to dive into them.

When he noticed his fingers clutching the menu too tightly, he forced himself to relax. After fifteen years, his feelings still had jagged, unfinished edges where Izzy was concerned.

"Are you ready to order?"

Distracted by his thoughts, Nate hadn't noticed the waitress's arrival. She filled their water glasses, then set the plastic pitcher on the table and stood looking down at them.

Her name tag read Willa, a good name for the petite, fair beauty whose long auburn waves and serene appearance made her look as if she'd emerged from another era.

Jack grinned at the waitress. "What's special today? Besides you?" Despite being married and having a houseful of children, he was obviously smitten.

Nate winced, but the woman remained unfazed, her cool expression revealing nothing as she responded. "We're serving a hot brisket sandwich on a kaiser roll. It comes with a side salad. The soup today is chicken in the pot."

Quickly Nate ordered the sandwich, hoping his friend would do the same without further embarrassing himself, but Jack had other plans. "I'll take the sandwich, and bring me a cold drink, too, gorgeous. 'Cause the more I look at you, the hotter I get."

"Jack," Nate began in a warning undertone, but the former Thunder Ridge Huskies football hero—emphasis on *former*—clearly thought he still had the goods.

Jack grinned at Nate. "You're in town awhile, right? Maybe Willa's got a friend, and we can double-date."

Willa picked up the pitcher of water, murmuring, "I'll get your sandwiches," but Jack, who had clearly lost his mind, patted the woman's butt, then reached for her wrist. The redhead tried to jerk away. Jack held on.

What came next happened so quickly Nate wasn't sure exactly what had occurred. He was aware of a voice hollering, "Hey!" and the next thing he knew, a large green… cucumber?…appeared at the table concurrent with a tidal wave of ice-cold water washing over him and Jack. Mostly Jack.

Jack yelled, the cucumber yelled back, and then it slipped in the puddle of water, falling in a heap of flailing green arms and legs.

"Pickle down!" a busboy shouted.

Ah, it was a pickle.

Nate rose to help.

"You threw that water on purpose," Jack accused.

"Shut up," Nate suggested as he knelt next to what appeared to be a life-size vegetable mascot. "Don't move," he said, unsure of where to check first for injuries. At least there was an abundance of padding. "Let's make sure you're not hurt before you try to get up."

Ignoring him, the irate dill pointed toward Jack. "You need to leave this restaurant. Now." Then it turned back to Nate. "And you. You—"

She stopped—it was definitely a she.

Half a lifetime fell away.

"Izzy?" Her name escaped on a rush of breath.

It took her longer to say his name, and when she did, her voice crackled. "Nate."

"You know her?" Jack glared. "She got water on my Wallabees." He raised a leg, pointing to his boot. "These are suede, man, and I haven't Scotchgarded them yet. I want to see the manager."

Because he found it impossible to break eye contact with Izzy, Nate felt rather than saw the small crowd that was gathering around them. He heard someone say, "She *is* the manager," and then people started talking over one another, their voices seeming distant and irrelevant.

Izzy.

That's what was relevant. The fact that Izzy Lambert was here, right where he'd left her—despite her avowal that she would leave this town someday and head for a big city with opportunities that were bigger and better than anything she'd known in Oregon.

"What happened?" he murmured.

"I slipped on the water."

He shook his head. Not what he'd meant. But he hadn't intended to speak his thought out loud, anyway.

He'd been told she left town and recalled his tangled

emotions at the time. It had taken some work, but he'd finally made peace with the fact that they'd been kids when they'd dated, that their relationship had been meant to last a summer not a lifetime and that, thankfully, the only people they'd truly hurt were themselves. Still, Izzy Lambert remained the big unanswered question of his life.

"Coming through. What happened here?"

Khaki-colored trousers appeared in Nate's peripheral vision. He glanced up to see a sheriff, who stood with his hands on his hips, looking amusedly down at Izzy.

"Izz. You hurt?"

"No."

"Okay. Up you go, then." The lawman, a big, good-looking guy, extended a hand.

"Wait a minute." Rising, Nate faced the sheriff. Now that he was standing, he realized the man was about his height…*maybe* a half inch taller…and roughly the same weight. Nate didn't like the slight smile around the other man's lips. "She shouldn't get up until we know for sure she hasn't broken something."

To the casual observer, the sheriff's smile appeared friendly, but there was a distinct challenge in the dark gaze that connected with Nate's.

"Sheriff Derek Neel." He introduced himself with a nod. No handshake. "And you are?"

Nate glanced at Izzy. Her eyes looked huge. "An old friend," he responded, not above a twinge of satisfaction when the sheriff's brow lowered a bit.

"Must be really old," Sheriff Neel surmised. "I've known Izz twelve years. I can't recall ever seeing you around."

It was Nate's turn to frown, and it felt more like a scowl. "Izz" must not have left Thunder Ridge for very long. She'd gone without getting in touch with him, without leaving a forwarding address. And back then she hadn't had email or a cell phone. Nate had already moved to Chicago to attend college, was already deeply immersed in that life. Other than phoning Henry to ask if he knew where Izzy was—and Henry had claimed he had no information about Izzy—there had been no way, really, to track her down.

Out of nowhere, the feelings he'd had half a lifetime ago came rushing back, brief but surprisingly powerful. The tight throat, the sick gut, the confusion, even the desire to punch something when he'd heard Izzy was gone—all those sensations were there again, despite the years and the experiences between then and now.

Izzy seemed frozen in place, but his glance unlocked her, and she struggled to sit up. The bulky costume impeded her efforts.

The sheriff grabbed her beneath the left elbow the same moment that Nate's fingers closed around her right arm. She looked at him, not at the other man, her eyes alarmed. Her soft, perfectly formed lips parted…and damned if he didn't feel it again—the old desire, the possessiveness he'd never felt about anyone or anything except Izzy Lambert.

She seemed to be primed to say "thank you," but no sound emerged. Instead, she stared back at him, breathing through her open mouth, silky brows arched, and he recalled the way she *used* to look at him, as if she'd been hungry for the very sight of him.

His glance dropped to her torso. Couldn't help it. Though he couldn't see it, he knew that beneath the bulky costume was the body he had gotten to know well. Too well, let's face it. He had seen it in sunlight, moonlight and the stark light of a doctor's office. He remembered it all.

Did she?

He shouldn't feel a damned thing for Izzy Lambert after all these years. Their relationship was a cold case. It had begun as a summer love and ended the way most everyone had predicted it would—with Nate leaving for college in another state and Izzy...

Well, he wasn't certain exactly what had happened to Izzy. All he knew for sure was that between the beginning and the end of their relationship, they had lived a lifetime, bonded in ways some couples never did. In one summer they had been forced to grow up, whatever innocence they'd once enjoyed gone for good. Maybe that was why the feelings weren't completely dead, at least not for him. In all the years since, he hadn't lived with that much intensity. Or passion.

With his blood feeling too hot for his veins, Nate wondered if he should have stayed away despite the passage of time. Then, just as suddenly, as if someone had turned on the air-conditioning, the heat of resentment cooled.

She'd planned to make a mark on the world, yet here she was: *a pickle.*

An angry pickle, coming to the defense of her coworker. Suddenly, he couldn't prevent the quirk of his lips. *Izzy, Izzy...* Somehow, the ridiculous situation suited her. She'd always been unpredictable, always surprising.

Nate glanced again at the sheriff. Who was he? Friend? Lover? Something more? Maybe. *But if she is, I wouldn't want to be in your boots, pal.* Izzy was still looking at him, not at the lawman.

Nate's relationship with Isabelle Lambert might be fifteen years dead and buried, but he could feel the current running between them right now, and suddenly Nate knew in his gut: returning to Thunder Ridge was either a mistake or the best decision he'd made in a long, long time.

Gridlock. That was the state of Izzy's brain.

Nate's fingers were wrapped around her upper arm as he and Derek lifted her to her feet. It might have taken one second or ten minutes. All she could feel was Nate… and fear.

His touch ignited a flash fire of memory. The years disappeared and once more she was standing between his arms, her back against his truck, feeling his heartbeat and his heat, inhaling the amazing, perfect scent of his skin as he pressed against her, his whisper warm in her ear: *"Do you know what the feel of you does to me?"* He'd been the only person who'd ever made her feel truly special. More than a decade later, parts of her body that had been in hibernation a long, long time suddenly woke up. That was not good.

To regain her composure, she tore her gaze from his. She needed time to think. Even after all the years of looking for him, of fearing she might run into him somewhere, he'd still managed to catch her completely off guard now that it had actually happened.

And then, the worst…

Big Ken, the affectionately named clock tower in front of City Hall, struck two. *Boom…boom…*

Oh, dear Lord. She didn't have much time at all. Seven minutes if she was lucky.

Her heart galloped as one thought rose above all others: *Get rid of him!*

"Nice to see you, Nate. I have to get back to work. Meal's on the house."

Izzy considered that a nice touch…friendly, but Nate's blue eyes narrowed. "We haven't eaten yet."

"Oh. Not a problem. We'll get you a sandwich to go."

Nate's frown deepened.

"You know what *I'd* like?" Jack, the jerk Izzy had seen groping Willa, stepped forward. "An apology for ruining my boots. Maybe even a reimbursement."

Izzy stared at the man. She'd caught him *fondling* her

employee, a woman so buttoned-up and proper that Izzy never told a blue joke in front of her.

Nate's friend was a big hulk of a guy. Izzy didn't recognize him, but she knew his type. Her mother had dated men like him: big, arrogant and dumb as rocks. Convinced you were as impressed with them as they were with themselves. *Forget the jerk. Get rid of Nate*, her brain counseled wisely. Her temper, however, which tended to get the best of her under stress, kindled.

"A reimbursement. Sure." She nodded. "Check's in the mail."

"All right. That's more like it."

"I was being facetious." Forgetting that from the neck down she was still dressed as a dill, she waddled up to the man to take him down a peg. "You know what *I* think? I think you need to apologize to Willa."

"To Willa?" Derek was beside her in a flash. "What happened?"

"Nothing!" Twisting a ring on her right hand, Willa shook her head. "It was all just a misunderstanding. It won't happen again."

"What won't happen again?" Derek squared off, ready for a showdown, which made Izzy realize instantly she should have kept her big mouth shut. Derek's history was dotted with confrontation, and he tended to be even more mulish than she.

"The lady said it was a misunderstanding." Nate stepped in. Unintimidated by Derek's badge, his stature or his expression, Nate spoke in a tone at once mildly appeasing and strongly cautionary. "Let's take her word for it. Jack, apologize to Willa."

Jack spoke up from safely behind his friend. "Why should *I* apologize?"

"To save your life." Nate tossed the wry reply over his

shoulder while maintaining eye contact with Derek, who now directed his glower toward Nate.

"Who are you again?" Derek demanded, his hands on his hips. "And how do you know Izzy?"

Izzy's heart began to pound. She and Nate had kept their personal business private. Because of her home life, Izzy had not socialized much, and because she and Nate had both had jobs, they'd reserved their limited time together strictly for each other. With the exception of Henry and Sam, who owned the deli and knew almost everything about her, most people had assumed she and Nate were just a fleeting high school crush. Here today, gone tomorrow. Which was exactly what she wanted them to assume.

I should use Gorilla Glue instead of lip gloss. If she'd kept her mouth shut, Nate and his friend might be out of here by now.

His gaze fell on her as he answered Derek. "Izzy and I are…old friends."

Was it her imagination, or had Nate hesitated a hair too long before he said "old friends"? In addition to Derek, half her crew had rushed over to help when she fell. She did not want to court their curiosity.

Addressing herself to Jack, she said, "Never mind. You know what? Check *is* in the mail."

"No, it's not." Nate turned toward her, his expression uncompromising. "He owes Willa—and you—an apology." The steadiness of his gaze made her skin prickle inside the hot costume.

"Whose side are you on?" Jack complained. "She got water on you, too, man."

Nate didn't glance his friend's way. His attention and low, intense words were all for Izzy. "Stand your ground, Isabelle. Don't let some jackass push you around."

"Hey!" Jack protested behind them.

Locked in a battle of gazes with Nate, anger blazed through Izzy like a brush fire.

Fifteen years ago, she would have given almost anything to have Nate Thayer on her side. To hear him stand up for her, stand up for *them*. But his supportive words were a decade and a half too late.

"You're giving me advice, Nate? No, thank you. What I want is for you to take your friend and go." She wasn't a weak, starry-eyed girl any longer. "I want you to go *right now.*" The last words were so choked, so intense, Nate may have been the only one to hear them.

The surprise on Nate's face offered a modicum of satisfaction. He seemed to be on the brink of saying something more before his expression shuttered, concealing his thoughts.

Slowly, he turned to his loudmouthed friend. "Apologize, and let's go."

"Apologize? For being friendly?"

"Do it," Nate said. "I'm sure the sheriff would like to kick your ass, Jack, and if he doesn't, I might. Stop arguing and start apologizing."

"Fine. Who do I have to apologize to? The cucumber or the waitress?"

Hands resting just above his gun belt, Derek got in Jack's face. "She's a pickle."

Nate shook his head. "Apologize to both of them," he ordered.

Face reddening, Jack turned first to Willa. "Okay. Sorry. I didn't mean anything by it." He raised his hand to show off the gold band. "I'm married." A resounding "ugh" circled through the small group of onlookers. Redder still, he looked at Izzy. "I apologize for making a big deal about the Wallabees. But they are new, and—"

Nate's hand clamped down firmly on Jake's shoulder.

"I think you can stop there." His gaze returned boldly to Izzy. He nodded. "Good to see you, Isabelle."

With her heart pounding against the foam costume, she gave a jerky nod.

He seemed to hesitate a moment longer, which made her nerves flare, then apparently deciding there was nothing else to say, he turned and walked toward the deli's glass door.

"Time to get back to work," she muttered, feeling slightly out of breath.

Her busboy Leon, and Oliver, the cook, returned to their jobs. Willa hurried after them.

Derek watched the petite redhead for several seconds, then looked at Izzy. His eyes narrowed. "Explanation, please. Who was that guy? 'Cause your face is as green as that ridiculous costume."

Chapter Two

"Shh." Izzy waved her hand, indicating that Derek should lower his booming voice. "I'll tell you later, I promise, but—" She stopped, her breath catching painfully in her throat.

As Nate and his friend reached the deli's entrance, a teenage boy pulled open the door.

Izzy's heart took off like a startled colt. For perhaps the second time in her life, she understood the term "blind panic." A cold sweat covered her body.

She wanted to run to the door, but her bones felt weak and rubbery, and she wouldn't know what to do once she got there. She watched helplessly as the boy held the door. Nate must have thanked him, because the teen smiled and nodded.

As Nate walked down the street, he glanced back through the broad window fronting the deli. Could he see far enough into the restaurant to note that she was still watching him? It seemed that he looked right at her before his friend drew his attention and they disappeared down the block.

"You look like you're going to be sick." Derek's voice boomed beside her. "What the hell is going on here today?"

"Not now." Her mouth was so dry, she could barely speak. "I'll tell you later, but—"

"Mom!"

Eli, her beautiful son, nearly as tall as she was now, with the same fair skin and straight brown hair as hers, loped toward them. The sight of his gangly body and broad smile never failed to make her feel as if she'd taken a hit of pure oxygen. Today the sight of him filled her with anxiety, too.

"Hey, Uncle Derek." Eli's speech was somewhat marred by the hearing impairment he had suffered as a baby.

"Hey, buddy."

"I'm staying," Eli announced, then used his expressive hands to sign the question *What's for dessert today?*

Instead of asking him whether he'd eaten lunch, Izzy both spoke and signed back, "There's strawberry cheesecake in the walk-in fridge. Help yourself."

Eli's eyes, hazel-green, like his mother's, widened in surprise. "Cool." She never offered him dessert before a healthful meal or, at the very least, a snack. Eli taught swim classes at the local parks and rec. She was always harping on him about healthful refueling. Now he trotted toward the kitchen, stopped and looked at her. *I had a sub sandwich with lettuce, tomato, spinach and pickles*, he signed. *In case you were wondering.* With a grin, Eli said hello to a waitress, dodged around her, then rounded the counter and disappeared into the kitchen calling, "Yo, O!" to Oliver, the lead cook, who had once bought Eli a set of child-sized saucepans and played "chef" with him for hours.

Oh, God, how she loved her little family. Nate's presence here could threaten everything she'd defied the odds to build.

"I'm on duty tonight," Derek said, keeping his voice low, "but I'll see you tomorrow. I expect a full debriefing."

He had never asked about Eli's father. Derek had too many of his own ghosts to request that Izzy dredge up hers, but once, during a vulnerable moment, she had told him a little bit about the summer she was seventeen.

"Tomorrow?" Derek had been a good friend for years, but would she be ready to tell him—or anyone—the truth by tomorrow night? Not likely. She needed time, time to find out how long Nate was going to be in town…time to figure out how to protect her son, because this wasn't just about her. "I'm…not sure I'm free tomorrow."

"What's the problem?" Derek asked. "You close at sundown on Friday nights."

"Yes, but I'm… I've got to… There's a very important—"

"Cut it out, Izz. You're a crap liar."

That's what you think. She chewed the inside of her lip.

Derek crossed his arms. "You're making me so curious I might stop by tonight on my shift."

"No." Eli would be home tonight. "Tomorrow," she relented.

Reappearing, Eli carried a plate of the deli's mile-high cheesecake. "This is the bomb," he said, pointing to it with his fork. Setting the plate aside so he had both hands free, he asked, *Mom, is it okay if I sleep at Trey's tonight? His dad said he'd drive us to Portland in the morning.*

Eli and his friend Trey were attending the same summer camp in Portland. After tonight, she wouldn't see him for two whole weeks.

"I can drive you." Glad to think of something other than Nate, she focused on the plans she'd already made. "I took the morning off. I thought we'd stop at Voodoo Doughnuts for maple-bacon bars." She smiled, for the moment just another mom trying to tempt her teenager into spending a little more time with her.

A flash of guilt crossed her son's features. Typically more comfortable with signing than oral speech when he had more than a few words to say, he used a combination of ASL and finger spelling to explain, *Trey's dad was a counselor for Inner City Project when he was our age. He's going to introduce us around.*

"Ah." For the past several summers, Eli had attended a camp for deaf kids. This summer, he'd insisted on "regular camp." The fourteen-year-old was the one thing in Izzy's life that had turned out absolutely, perfectly right. Refraining, with difficulty, from telling him he was already way, way better than "regular," Izzy had spent more money than she should have to register Eli for the camp with Trey.

"Traveling with Trey and Mr. Richards sounds like a great idea," she said. "You have a good time. In fact, I'll take off early and help you pack."

I'm already packed. I can sleep at Trey's so we can get an early start tomorrow. His mom invited me to dinner.

"Oh. Well…great. Great, because I wasn't even sure what to make tonight." His favorite monster burritos, actually. *Have a fabulous time, First Mate,* she signed without speaking.

Aye, aye, Skipper, he signed back, playing along with the endearments they'd been using since he was in third grade and they'd eaten their dinners at the coffee table, watching reruns of *Gilligan's Island.* She probably ought to stop calling him cutesy names that would make a less patient kid gag.

I'll see you in a couple of weeks, Mom. He looked at Derek. *Take care of her for me, Uncle Derek.*

Derek both signed and spoke back, "I'll do that, buddy."

Eli made a move toward his mother, then looked uncertain. *I'm not sure how to hug you when you're a pickle.*

Solving the problem, she tossed her arms around her

son, gave him a warm squeeze, then began to run through the list of safety precautions he needed to take at camp.

Eli nodded for a while before interrupting, *Mom, I got the memo. Literally.* He looked at Derek and splayed his fingers. "She wrote five pages."

Izzy blushed. "It's easy to forget things when you're away."

Mom, I'll be safe, respectful and aware of my surroundings. I won't lose my hearing aid, 'cause it's really *expensive, and I'll be back in two weeks with all my body parts.* And then, just so she would have a memory to reduce her to tears every day that he was away, Eli kissed her on the cheek and said with his most careful enunciation, "See you, Skipper."

She refused to cry. Until he was out the door.

After exchanging a manly hug with Derek, Eli jogged out of the deli. Izzy didn't start sniffling audibly until the glass door closed behind her only child, leaving her with her worries and a sense of loneliness that made her feel hollow as an empty tomb.

"Aw, come on, Pickle. He'll be home soon." Derek's arm went round her in what turned out to be a kind of stranglehold. "Do you know pickles have no visible shoulders? Makes it hard to be friendly." He adjusted his arm a bit more companionably. "If I wasn't on duty tonight, I'd keep you company. I'll bring pizza tomorrow. The works?"

"Sure."

Willa walked by carrying a lox platter, and Derek's attention instantly swerved to the petite redhead. "For pity's sake, ask her out already," Izzy whispered. "You stare at her every time you come in."

"She doesn't stare back."

Izzy shook her head, content to focus on someone else's fears instead of her own for a while. "Sheriff Neel, are you telling me a big, strapping lawman like you is afraid of a tiny, little woman who hasn't uttered an unkind word since she's been here?"

Derek grunted.

"When was the last time you went on a date?" she needled. "You can't be a sheriff 24/7, buddy. You need a reason to wear street clothes once in a while."

One of Derek's brows arched. "Look who's talking. You're a pickle. How's your date card these days, Isabelle? Do I need to find someone else to watch *Shark Tank* with?"

The last time Izzy had felt motivated to take a good hard look at her love life, she'd wound up alone in the back office, eating a quart of matzo ball soup and putting a sizable dent in a chocolate chip babka. "Fine. Never mind," she muttered. "I was trying to be helpful." She and Derek lapsed into grumpy silence for several seconds, disgusted far more with themselves than with each other.

Finally, Derek spoke. "If you need something before tomorrow, call me. I mean, with the kid leaving."

She nodded. "Thanks. I better get back to work,"

"Me, too. Lives to protect and all that."

"Yeah. Pickles to serve."

With one last, not-very-subtle glance at Willa, he headed toward the coatrack at the front of the deli, where he'd hung his hat.

Izzy sighed. All right, so they were both terminally pathetic when it came to romance. At least Derek had a town to watch over, and she—

I have a restaurant and a family to save. Here in this dying deli were people she loved who loved her back. That was something. More, in fact, than she'd ever thought she would have. She intended to protect what was hers, no matter what.

First, though, she had to get out of this pickle suit, which felt like a personal sauna, and go somewhere alone so she could think clearly.

Waddling to the counter, she told Audra, who had worked at the deli longer than she had, "I'm leaving for a couple of hours. If you can hold down the fort, I'll be back in plenty of time for the dinner shift." Without Eli at home, she'd be better off working instead of worrying. Maybe if she took a break, she could figure out what to do about Nate Thayer and the child they'd made together.

"We can do this, no problem," Izzy grunted, standing on the pedals of her bike. "Going uphill is good…for…us." Her teeth ground together. Every downstroke was harder to come by than the one before as she pumped determinedly up Vista Road. "We're going to start…doing this…every… day," she panted to her beloved dog, Latke, a Shar-Pei rescue whose ambivalence toward physical activity gave credence to the distinction *nonsporting breed*.

Her heart and head both thudded painfully, but even that was better than the avalanche of questions that buzzed in her brain on the heels of Nate Thayer's return. So far, she had not a single answer, not even a clue as to what was going to happen if and when her son discovered that his father was in Thunder Ridge…or vice versa.

Nausea and dizziness the likes of which she hadn't experienced since she was pregnant overwhelmed her. Eli had questioned her about his father a few times, mostly during the tween years when his own identity was in minute-by-minute flux. The answers she'd provided hadn't been satisfying, but at least they had cooled Eli's incessant wondering about the man whose life goals had not included a pregnant teenage girlfriend.

"'Kay, I think I'm going to puke now."

She had to stop pedaling, hop off the seat and close her eyes. Latke accepted the rest stop as an opportunity to prostrate herself in the bike lane.

Izzy leaned over the handlebars. "We'll get going in a sec, baby, just as soon as Mama's heart attack is done."

"Would rehydrating help?"

On a fresh surge of adrenaline, Izzy's eyes popped open. A clear plastic water bottle, icy cold with condensation dripping down the sides, dangled in front of her.

"Bike much?" Nate Thayer arched a brow, lips twisting sardonically.

Silently cursing fate, Izzy stared at him. She had deliberately ridden away from town and in the opposite direction from the dairy farm where Nate had grown up. "What are you doing out here?" The question sounded like an accusation.

"Tsk, tsk, tsk." He shook his head. "We need to polish our welcome committee skills. This is the second time in one day that you haven't greeted me on my return home."

"Home?" Izzy felt as if a giant fist were squeezing her stomach. "You're here to stay?" Her distaste for that possibility was clear as a bell and drew a deep frown from Nate.

Unscrewing the top of the water bottle, he held it out again. "Take it. You're about to keel over."

"No, I'm not."

A smile tugged his lips. "Take it anyway."

Willing her fingers to stop shaking, Izzy plucked the bottle from his hand, careful not to touch him. Lowering the kickstand, she stepped away from her bike with Nate observing her every move. Even when she stopped looking at him, she could feel his eyes on her, the way she used to sense him watching her in the deli fifteen years ago. Back then her skin would tingle with excitement, even as she'd pretended not to notice. Today, anxiety made her skin prickle like needle pokes.

She bent toward her dog. "Here, sweetie." Tilting Nate's offering, she let Latke drink. The Shar-Pei's heavy jowls flapped as she slurped with the grace of a hippo sipping from a martini glass.

During the summer that she and Nate had been a couple, Izzy had never truly confronted him. How could she? She had been so besotted, so damn *grateful* that the high school heartthrob had chosen her, a girl with an embarrassing family and no prospects for a decent future. Now, when her dog was finished drinking, she stood and met Nate's gaze with challenge in her own. "Latke says thanks."

He addressed her dog. "You're welcome."

Wearing the same clothes he'd had on in the deli—J.Crew jeans and a sea-blue V-necked T-shirt that matched his eyes almost identically (yeah, she'd noticed), his hair still ridiculously thick and shiny—he shrugged. "I only brought the one bottle. Come back to my room. There's more water in the minibar."

Izzy glanced in the direction from which Nate had come. The heavily shingled roof of the Eagle's Crest Inn peeked through a grove of pine trees. "How did you even see me from the inn? " she asked.

"My room faces the street. And my desk faces the window. When I saw you crawl by, I thought, 'Well, what do you know? Fate must want us to have a reunion, even if Izzy doesn't.'" His gaze narrowed. "It's been a long time. You must have a few minutes to spare for an old friend."

There it was, the liquid velvet voice that used to make her feel as if she were wrapped in the most comfortable blanket ever created.

"I haven't, actually. I'm due back at the deli." Shoving the empty bottle into the saddlebag on her bike, she climbed back on and tried to tug sixty pounds of wrinkled canine to a standing position. "Let's go, girl." No movement.

"I think she needs a nap."

What her pet needed was a couple thousand volts. "She's

fine. She loves to run. Let's go, Latke." Izzy put her right foot on the bike pedal, intending to pull the dog into a standing position if she had to. She jerked with surprise when Nate clamped his fingers around the handlebars.

He leaned forward, his shadow looming over her. Humor fled his expression, replaced by curiosity and displeasure. "If I didn't know better, Isabelle, I'd say you plan to avoid me until I leave town. Why?"

"That's not my intention at all. I'm just very busy right now. I'm sure we'll find time before you go. When did you say you're leaving?"

"I didn't say."

"Well, I'm sure we'll run into each other again. And now I know where you're staying, so…" She tried to back the bike up, but he was still holding her handlebars.

"So you'll get in touch?" His voice grew quiet, penetrating. "I should expect a call? Like last time?"

"Last time." Izzy's stomach began to twist so hard she wanted to double over. "What do you mean?"

"When I went to Chicago, you and I agreed to talk once a week. Then suddenly you were gone, no forwarding address, no warning."

Threads of anger wove through Izzy's fear. "No warning? Yeah, I suppose you're right. I should have told you all about my plans. Ten minutes once a week wasn't a lot of time, though. I'd have to talk really fast."

"I'm not following you."

"You're not? Every Sunday afternoon," she reminded him, "from five to five ten Pacific Time? Nate Thayer's obligatory check-in to the girl he'd knocked up back in Oregon. Very thoughtful, those calls, but you have to admit they didn't leave a lot of time to talk about anything in depth." Which, she had thought at the time, must have been the point.

Surprise hijacked Nate's features, and Izzy took the

opportunity to wrest the handlebars from his grip. He moved in front of the bike immediately. "That's what you thought I was doing? Just fulfilling an obligation?"

"That *is* what you were doing. Look, Nate," Izzy chided, "it's ancient history, but let's not rewrite it. When I got pregnant, you saw your college dreams flushing down the toilet. So, you and your parents came up with a solution— put the baby up for adoption and check in with the pregnant teenager once a week to make sure she's still on board. Perfectly logical. Frankly, if I'd had a scholarship to a big university and parents who'd already picked out the frame for my diploma, I might have felt the same way."

"You agreed that adoption seemed like the best solution."

"I was seventeen, pregnant and dead broke. I wasn't in a great position to argue."

Nate's brows swooped low. A muscle tensed in his jaw. "Are you saying you didn't want to put the baby up for adoption?"

Her mind began to race like a machine that was out of control—couldn't slow down, couldn't stop.

"You agreed we were both too young to be good parents," he said, glancing at a car that whizzed by. "I don't want to discuss this on the street. Why don't you come up—"

"I don't want to discuss this at all." She made a show of looking at her watch. "I have to go." When she tried to push the bike forward, however, Nate held on.

A sharp burning sensation rose behind Izzy's eyes. *Don't cry. Don't you dare cry, not after all this time.* But she remembered one occasion—just the one—when Nate had stopped being logical and reasonable about how they were too young and too uneducated and not financially able to raise a baby properly. On that single occasion, before he'd left for college, his brow had hitched in the middle like it was right now, worry muddying the usually clear and confident expression in his eyes, and he'd said, "Do you think it'll be a boy or a girl?"

In that one moment, they had felt like parents, not two kids who had made a colossal mistake.

She swallowed hard.

"You know what I remember, Nate? I remember what your mother and father said—that our relationship was 'a lapse in good judgment.' And that we'd be crazy to throw our futures away." They had meant their son's future, of course. There hadn't been many people around at that time who'd held out much hope for her future. "We shouldn't blame each other for anything. It might have been different if we'd loved each other, right? But we were just kids." Her sad smile was the genuine article. "You're lucky you had parents who were looking out for you."

"Izzy—"

"I really do have to go now."

Using the heel of her running shoe to flip the kickstand, Izzy climbed aboard her bike and pushed forward toward Latke, urging her to fall into step. Nate watched her every move but didn't try to stop her this time as she checked for traffic and made a U-turn on Vista Road.

Traveling downhill, Izzy went as fast as she dared push her trotting dog, desperate to outrun worry and the tears that, finally, would not be denied. She swiped the back of her hand across her nose and used her palm to wipe her eyes. Determined to keep the details of her home life private when she was younger, she'd kept to herself in middle and high school, flying as far under the radar as possible and even earning the nickname "Loner Chick." After a while, she'd been largely ignored, which had been fine by her. She'd never traded one word with Nate Thayer until the summer after he'd graduated.

What a tangled web she had woven when she, a girl from as far over the wrong side of the tracks as you could get, fell in love with the golden boy of Thunder Ridge. And got pregnant.

That hadn't been her biggest sin, though. No, not by a long shot. Her biggest sin had been believing Nate loved her back, that he would change his mind about the baby and that they would live happily ever after. Her biggest sin had been telling herself the lie that when you loved hard enough, all your dreams would come true.

Chapter Three

For Izzy, "home" was the one-word description of the blood, sweat and tears she had put into constructing not just a building but a family. The deli had been her first real home, and she had happily painted its aged walls, twisted new washers onto leaking faucets and waxed its linoleum tiles until the memory of their former luster glinted through the wear and tear.

It was the same with the cottage in which she and Eli made their home. When she'd first laid eyes on the 860-square-foot space, her heart had sunk. The tiny house was all she'd been able to afford and even then she'd had to borrow the down payment (paid back in full) from her boss Henry, who by that time had become more of a surrogate father to her.

The prospect of owning her own home, a place she and her son could call theirs forever, had pushed her to overlook the dark wood walls, the ugly threadbare carpets and the cracked enamel in the ancient claw-foot tub, not to mention the spaces in the roof shingles through which she could actually see the sky. Izzy and Eli, who by then had turned seven, dubbed the little house Lambert Cottage, and she'd learned all she could about repairs and improvements.

Today their home was a sunny, whitewashed space with a scrubbed pine floor she'd discovered beneath the carpets, and pale pear-green furniture she'd reupholstered on her own. She made Thanksgiving dinners in her tiny kitchen and hosted birthday parties in a garden filled with azalea, honeysuckle and lydia broom. It was no longer possible to see sky through the roof, but there were times late at night as Izzy lay in bed saying her prayers that she gazed into the darkness above her head and was sure she could see heaven. Coming home never, ever failed to soothe and reassure her.

Except this afternoon.

Unleashing Latke, she set out a bowl of fresh water, chugged a tumbler of iced tea, rinsed her glass and set it upside down on the wooden drain rack, just as she would have done on any normal day. The difference was that today her hands shook the entire time, and she thought she might throw up.

Since she'd pedaled away from Nate, memories had been buffeting her so hard she felt like a tiny dinghy on a storm-ridden sea. Some of the memories were good. So good that yearning squeezed her heart like a sponge. Others were more bittersweet. But there was one memory that rose above the others, whipping up a giant wall of emotion that threatened to capsize her: the recollection of the day she'd accepted that the boy she loved was never going to love her back, not the same way, and that she'd rather be alone the rest of her life than beg for a love that wasn't going to come...

Fifteen years earlier...

Nate ran his fingers through his hair—that famously thick black hair—then remained head down, elbows on knees, hands cradling his forehead. "Damn it."

Izzy winced at the frustration in his tone, wondering if he was directing it at her, at the news she'd just given him or at both. Probably both. What hurt the most, she thought, was that the best summer of her life was now quite clearly the worst of his. "I'm sorry."

What a stupid thing to say! Plus, she'd whispered the words, which made the fact that she'd apologized even worse.

She was no wimp. But sitting next to Nate on a bench in Portland's Washington Park, exhausted and freaking terrified, she figured that if *I'm sorry* was the best she could do, then so be it. Seventeen had felt so much older and more mature just a week ago. Tonight she felt like a little girl afraid of the dark and of the unknown.

"You're positive?" Nate demanded. His voice, which had always made her think of soft, dark velvet, tonight sounded more like a rusty rake scraping cement.

Izzy nodded. She was "positive," all right. She'd bought four early-pregnancy tests, which had sucked up three hours' worth of income from her job waiting tables at The Pickle Jar deli. Every single test had turned up a thin pink line. She'd never liked pink.

"I'm pregnant," she confirmed. *May as well get used to saying it out loud.*

"How?" Raising his head, Nate looked at the evening skyline beyond the Rose Test Garden, where they sat, rather than at her.

How? *How* was obvious, right? They'd been having sex since May. Nearly four full months of his waiting for her when she got off work at the restaurant and then whisking her away in his old Toyota pickup. It could have been a limousine or a horse-drawn carriage—that was how lucky Izzy had felt to be driving into the night with Nate Thayer.

"I mean, we used protection," Nate said now, trying to reason out her news. "Every time."

Hardly the words of comfort—and solidarity—she'd been hoping for.

Suck it up, Izz. He's shocked.

A year older and already graduated from high school, Nate had plans for his life…so did she…plans that did not include becoming a teenage parent.

"Not every time," she countered.

"What?"

"Protection. We didn't use it *every* time. Not on the Fourth of July."

"The Fourth? Yes, we—" He stopped. And swore again.

Her heart, which for the past few months had felt as if it were unfolding like one of the roses in Washington Park, suddenly shriveled around the edges.

They'd made love in the bed of his truck nearly two months ago on Independence Day, atop a thick pile of sleeping bags. With most of the people in their hometown watching the fireworks down at the river, she and Nate had agreed to keep their romance as private as possible. Izzy hadn't wanted to invite prying eyes or unwelcome comments. So on that Fourth of July, they'd driven to the resort where he'd worked over the summer. Parked near a small lake, with Santana cranked up on the radio, Nate had gazed down at her. The lights in the distance had illuminated his face—so beautiful, so serious. Wondering at his expression, she'd touched his cheek, and he'd whispered, almost as if he was surprised, "I feel better with you than I do anyplace else."

Her love had exploded like the fireworks.

"Are you sure it's mine?"

Sudden and sharp, the question plunged into Izzy's chest with the force of a dagger. Her gaze fused with his and she saw the truth in his eyes, so obvious that she couldn't catch her breath: he hoped another boy could be the baby's father.

Suddenly, the scent of spent blooms from the end-of-summer roses became overwhelming. Running for the cover of the bushes, Izzy retched into the ground.

While her stomach surrendered its contents, her mother's words from earlier this summer tumbled through her brain.

"Running off with that hottie? If you're smart, you'll get knocked up. Then maybe you can get him to take care of you." Felicia had punctuated her advice by raising her beer can in a mock toast. *"It never lasts, but it's better than nothing."*

On her way out the door—yes, she had *been going to meet Nate—Izzy had turned to give the woman who'd only sort of raised her a withering glare. "I would never do that. I'm not like you."*

Genuine laughter had erupted around the cigarette Felicia had put between her lips. "Oh, sweetie, you are exactly like me. The only difference is you think it's classier to give it away for free." As Izzy slammed the screen door, Felicia's words tagged after her. "You're going to wind up like me, too. Count on it."

It took Izzy a while to realize that Nate was beside her, one hand smoothing her light brown curls from her face, the other supporting her shoulders as she bent over the ground.

"I don't want your help." With her forearm, she knocked his hand away. Nate reared back in surprise.

Of course he was surprised. Up to now, she'd never been anything but sweet and agreeable. She'd been so happy, so grateful to be with him.

"Hey!" He grabbed her arm when she attempted to rise

on her own. "Stop. You're going to make yourself sick again. Just relax a minute."

"Relax?" Was he serious? "Good idea. Maybe I'll sign up for prenatal yoga. I'm pretty sure Ridge High offers that senior year."

Nate rubbed both hands down his face. "Okay, look, I was being an ass when I asked if it was mine. I'm sorry. I don't… I don't know how to do this, Izzy. No one has ever told me she was pregnant before."

"Well, that makes two of us, because I've never said it before."

He nodded. Then, ignoring her protest, he put his arm firmly around her waist and led her back to the bench. Finding a napkin in the picnic basket she'd packed for them, he wiped her brow. His touch and the fact that he insisted on helping her was sweet torture. She'd spent her whole life relying on herself, no longer daring to hope for one person she could lean into until she'd met Nate. When he collapsed against the bench, not making physical contact with her, she had to fight the urge to scoot closer.

He stretched his neck up, as if searching for an answer in the dark sky. "I'm supposed to leave for college in two weeks," he said.

"I know." He had told her from the beginning, and lately she'd hoped… Never mind what she'd hoped.

Don't panic. Panicking won't help.

"I've got to tell my parents." He sounded as if he was about to tell them he'd found out he was dying.

"Maybe they'll be supportive."

Nate's laugh told her otherwise. "Izzy, my father works twelve-hour days on a dairy farm and moonlights as a handyman so I can have a college fund. My mom taught piano and cleaned hotel rooms to pay for my after-school sports fees, because she thought it would help me get a scholarship. You think they're going to enjoy hearing this?"

"Don't yell at me, I didn't get pregnant alone!"

"I know that!" His energy felt explosive as he rose from the bench. "I'm just saying this changes everything. Not only for us. For other people."

"I can get a full-time job," she said, hearing the desperation in her voice. "I can work while you go to school, so—"

"You can't support three people."

"You said you were going to work while you're in college."

He nodded. "I've got to help with tuition and books." He shoved his fingers through his hair. "If I'm lucky, I'll have enough left over for living expenses."

"I can pay my own way. I have for years. I don't expect you to—"

"Izzy! Who's going to take care of the baby while you and I are in school and at work and studying? I'm going to college in Chicago. We'd be two thousand miles away from anyone we know. No," he said when she opened her mouth to protest. On a giant exhalation, he plowed both hands through his hair, then moved as if he were slogging through thigh-deep sand to sit beside her.

An anchor of fear pulled at Izzy's heart. Looking at the Portland skyline, she blinked as the city lights blurred. *No tears. Absolutely no tears.*

They didn't live in this sprawling city. Both she and Nate were from a Ridge community three and a half hours away. They'd come to Portland to soak up a view that was a taste of the bigger life awaiting them.

He was going to build skyscrapers.

She had planned to be the first person in her family to earn a high school diploma and go on to college.

Suddenly, Izzy felt as if nothing was holding her upright, as if she might slide off the bench. Stiffening her spine, she sat side by side with him—silently and with space between their bodies, which had not been their way this summer. The August evening felt hot and oppressive.

At the point where the silence was about to become unbearable, Nate spoke again. This time he sounded like someone who'd been running in the desert. "We'll figure it out. I'll talk to my parents. There's got to be something… We'll figure it out together." Nate's large palm and beautiful long fingers curved around the hands she clutched on her lap. Chancing a look at him, Izzy saw that he was staring at the ground.

The warmth that usually flooded her body when he touched her did not come.

Not once in four months had Nate actually said the words *I love you*. Izzy had counseled herself to be patient. Told herself she didn't have to hear the words to believe he felt them.

She shook her head. *Stupid…stupid!* How could a girl like her possibly know what love looked like?

With the rose-colored glasses off, the truth became painfully clear. Now, even though she was right next to Nate, even though he'd said they would find a solution together, she felt the heart that had warmed and softened this summer turn as cold and hard as stone.

"So the waitress says to the man at the counter, 'We have two soups today, sir, chicken with noodles and split pea—both delicious. Which would you like?' And the customer says, 'I'll take the chicken.' But, after the waitress calls in the order, the man changes his mind. 'Miss,' he asks, 'is it too late to switch? I think I'd prefer the split pea.' 'Not at all,' the waitress replies, and she turns around and hollers to the cook, 'Hold the chicken, make it pee!'"

Henry Bernstein leaned back in the guest chair in The Pickle Jar's tiny office and smiled the sweet, mischievous smile that usually warmed Izzy down to her toes. Henry had told her at least one new joke every week for the past seventeen years. At seventy-six years young, he liked to claim he knew more jokes than a professional comic.

"Where'd you hear that one?" Izzy tried to smile, but she wasn't up to her usual hearty laughter.

"I spent a week with two hundred senior citizens." Henry shrugged. "It's a laugh a minute in those retirement homes. Lots of company, three meals a day and all the Bengay you want. Not a bad life."

Henry and his younger brother, Sam, had just returned from visiting their friend Joe Rose, who lived at Twelve Oaks, a senior residence along the Willamette River. "I'm glad you enjoyed it, but I'm even gladder you're back," Izzy told him sincerely. "It's never the same around here without you. And I hope you're ready to get back to work, because I've been putting together some marketing ideas. I think I know how we can pump up business."

Raising the elegant, elderly hands that had scooped pickles out of an oak barrel back in the day, Henry said, "In a minute, in a minute. First, tell me what's so awful that you haven't been sleeping."

"Who says I haven't been sleeping?"

"Your eyes tell me. Is it business that's keeping you awake, Izzy girl? Remember—" He raised a finger. "'Tension is who you think you should be—relaxation is who you are.'"

Now she did laugh. "You heard that from someone at the retirement home. Only someone retired would say it."

"It's an ancient Chinese proverb."

"Written by a *retired* ancient Chinese prophet."

Henry grinned.

"Business isn't all that's keeping me up at night," she admitted. In her life, she'd had only one person to whom she could turn with any problem, and that was the thin, wise, gray-haired man in front of her.

"Nate Thayer," Izzy said, speaking the name aloud for the first time since yesterday afternoon. She'd avoided it, as if not saying his name might make his presence less real. "He's here, in Thunder Ridge. He came to the deli yesterday. He saw Eli."

Henry was rarely given to quick or exaggerated expressions, but now his brows arched above the line of his glasses. "He knows?"

"No. He didn't recognize Eli. And Eli had no idea, of course. He held the door open for Nate. They smiled at each other."

"But you and Nate spoke?"

"Yeah. I was wearing the pickle costume, and I fell on the floor, and— Never mind." Shaking her head, she pressed her fingers to her temples. "It was awkward."

Henry folded his hands above his belt line and nodded. "I thought he would come back someday."

Too agitated to sit still, Izzy rose, wrapping her arms around her middle as if it was nineteen degrees outside instead of close to ninety. "He took his time. Not that I'm complaining. I wish he'd never come back. I wish I didn't have to think about Nate Thayer again until Eli is an adult."

"Did he come here looking for information?"

"I don't know. He hasn't asked anything yet. But he's not entitled to information." Henry gazed at her. "He's *not*," she insisted before Henry could share some ancient wisdom about fathers' rights—fathers who hadn't wanted to raise their children to begin with.

"Nate and his parents wanted me to put our baby up for adoption. He was willing to wait until Eli was eighteen before he ever saw him. So let him wait a little longer."

"You're worried," Henry said, nodding. "It's understandable. But you're speaking out of fear."

"You're darn right I am." The tiny office didn't leave much room for pacing, but Izzy made use of the space that was available. "You remember how Eli was a few years ago. His self-esteem was terrible. He hated everything about himself, including the fact that he had a father who didn't want him." She had never told Eli that, of course, never even hinted, but short of lying and saying that the man who had fathered him died or was living in Tunisia, what else could a father's absence in his son's life imply? She had told him only that his father was a boy she had known. A boy who hadn't been ready to be a father and who had moved far away. Eli had never asked for a name, an act of self-control that seemed to give him a sense of power. He had referred to the man who'd fathered him once as "the guy with the Y chromosome." Then he'd stopped talking about it all together.

"He's on the right track now," she said emphatically. "He's a good student. Responsible and productive. He's happy. I intend to keep him feeling good about himself. I won't allow Nate to waltz in here and mess up my son's life."

Behind wire-rimmed glasses, Henry's brown eyes watched her closely. "Eli *is* on the right track. And circumstances are very different now. Eli was also upset about being deaf in a hearing world. The cochlear implant made a great difference."

"Yes. Because being able to hear took his mind off what he doesn't have. He never talks about not having a father anymore. It doesn't make him unhappy now. He has you, and Sam and Derek. He knows you love him."

"And always will. That doesn't mean he's stopped wondering, dear heart."

"Of course not. That's not what I mean. I've never underestimated how much Eli would want a father. You know that," she insisted. "But he's finally focusing on what he does have, not on what he doesn't." She looked at Henry hopefully, seeking his consensus.

Sun-weathered brow puckering, Henry removed his

bifocals and began to clean them with his shirttail. Izzy opened a desk drawer, withdrew a tiny spray bottle and cloth she kept just for Henry and Sam, then wiped the lenses until they were clear before returning them to him. "As far as Nate and his parents know," she said quietly, "I went through with the adoption plan. Nate's never gotten in touch to ask for information before. In all likelihood, he's come back to town for a reason that has absolutely nothing to do with us. If he does find out about Eli, and still has no interest in contact or in being a father..." She shuddered, the possibility too awful to contemplate.

Growing up unwanted left scars you could hide but not heal. Izzy knew that from experience and would do anything to protect her son from the miserable feeling that he wasn't good enough to be loved. It was far, far better to accept reality than to hope for a love that would never come.

"I still remember the day you told me you wanted to leave Thunder Ridge so you could have the baby somewhere else," Henry said. "I didn't want you to go. The thought of you being alone in a strange city..." He shook his head. "You were so young."

"Well, I wasn't alone. Joanne was wonderful."

Henry and his late wife had had a friend named Joanne, who'd been recently widowed, and Henry had offered to contact the woman about Izzy. Joanne had been happy to have the company of a quiet, studious seventeen-year-old... even a quiet, studious, four-months-pregnant seventeen-year-old. Izzy had been able to leave Thunder Ridge with most people, including her own mother, unaware that she was even pregnant.

Joanne and Izzy had gotten along so well that Joanne had invited her to stay on in Portland after the baby was born. She'd watched Eli while Izzy had attended community college and worked. She'd taught a teenager how to care for a baby.

A little more than three years later, Izzy had returned with an associate degree, a baby and no one any the wiser that Nate was the father. People had seemed to accept her story that the baby's father was someone she'd met in Portland.

"I'm still grateful that you introduced me to Joanne. She's wonderful," Izzy told Henry. She and the older woman were still in touch, and Izzy visited with Eli when she could.

"She's grateful, too." Henry nodded, but his brow furrowed, making Izzy wonder what was coming next. "Nate *did* call after you left for Portland," he reminded her. "He sounded worried. He wanted very much to talk to you. In the back of my mind, I've always wondered what would have happened if I'd told him you changed your mind and were keeping the baby."

"Nothing!" Izzy answered swiftly, her pulse speeding. "Nothing good would have happened. He'd already made his decision. If you had told him I was keeping the baby, he'd have sicced his parents on me again, so they could make me change my mind, and I was stressed enough without that."

Insisting that adoption was the only sensible solution to the "problem" of Izzy's pregnancy, Nate's parents had argued their point of view convincingly. The Thayers were blue-collar folks who had worked day and night, literally, to ensure that their son's life would be easier than their own. Wasn't Izzy also eager for a better life? Didn't she, too, want to attend college? And if she truly cared about Nate, how would she feel watching the plans for his future slip away? Those were some of the arguments they had used to convince her everyone's life would be ruined unless she put the baby up for adoption.

At first Izzy had allowed them to persuade her, and Nate had gone to college believing Izzy agreed with the adoption plans and assured by his parents that they would "watch over" Izzy during her pregnancy. And they had.

Mrs. Thayer had accompanied her to an ob-gyn in Bend, far enough away that no one in Thunder Ridge would know what was going on. Then his mother had made an appointment with an adoption lawyer, too, and had sat beside Izzy, holding her hand, throughout the first visit. No "mother" had held her hand before.

And so Izzy had done what she had sworn to herself she absolutely would not do again: she had hoped. She had begun to believe the Thayers liked her, that the baby was becoming real to them, as it was to her. Surely this caring—this is what family did for one another.

And Nate's weekly check-in calls...

At first, she had excused the fact their duration was brief and the content superficial. After all, the first weeks of college were busy and stressful. He would tell her a bit about his life when she asked him specific questions and he would ask her how she was feeling—whether she was eating right, if she was able to keep up with senior year homework. That, along with his parents' interest, had been enough for her to begin dreaming again...

Maybe Nate would miss her and ask her to come to Chicago...

His parents would realize they couldn't give up their first grandbaby...

She would prove that she could become a mother and support Nate's studies and eventually his career, and someday the Thayers—and Nate—would look back and thank God that Izzy and her child were part of the family.

Welcome to fantasyland, Izzy thought now, *where we pay no attention to pesky details like* reality.

She had Mrs. Thayer to thank for setting her straight. With crystal clarity, she'd shown Izzy that Nate did not want her or her baby.

So in her fourth month of pregnancy, Izzy had left town, telling the Thayers she preferred to handle the adoption on her own, without their help, and that they could pass that information along to Nate, since she had no desire to see him again.

"I gave Nate's parents exactly the out they were hoping for," she said to Henry. "It was better for everyone's sake to let them think they were getting what they wanted. The truth wouldn't have changed the outcome anyway. It just would have created more tension and fighting."

For a moment, Henry looked as if he wanted to argue, but how could he? They both remembered exactly how Nate's family had felt about her. She had reminded them of everything they had worked so hard to rise above.

"Eli will be at camp for two weeks," she reminded Henry. "I'm not sure how long Nate plans to be in town, but he is not entitled to any information that could hurt Eli in the long run." As she spoke, she began to feel stronger. "Our policy has got to be don't ask, don't tell. Eli has me. He has you and Sam and Derek and everyone else at the deli. He knows you all love him and accept him exactly as he is. If he wants to look for his father when he's eighteen, that's his prerogative. Until then, it's my job to protect him." That had been her purpose all these years. "The Thayers wanted perfection—a son with a degree, six figures a year and a perfect family. Eli and I will never fit that mold."

Henry shook his head. "You talk about what his parents wanted, but what did Nate want, dear heart?"

She smiled at the endearment. *Dear heart.* God had been good to her: despite her false starts, she'd been given a family. She answered Henry's question honestly. "Nate wanted the life he planned before he met me." She shrugged, way past the grief that had once consumed her. "We really were too young. If nothing else, the Thayers were right about that. Nate was a college-bound jock looking for a light-hearted summer romance, and I was a desperate, love-hungry teen."

"You're too hard on yourself."

Izzy shrugged, unconcerned. "Maybe."

Taking her seat, she fired up the computer. She had fought for the life she now lived, and it was a good one, built on hard work and a stern levelheadedness. She didn't try to fool herself anymore.

Did she ever want more than she already had? Yes, sure. Sometimes. It was only natural that deep in the night, she would occasionally wish for a hand she could curl her fingers around, a bare foot to bump into, someone to hold her and make her feel warm again when life's relentless everyday worries left her cold. But in those hungry, vulnerable moments, she would picture Eli as an adult—tall and strong, confident and self-accepting, pursuing a career he was passionate about and maybe starting a family of his own—and that would keep her on her path.

Right now, she needed to get back to business. Business was always a safe harbor.

She knew Henry would be pleased with some of the ideas she'd had while he was on vacation. Tapping on her keyboard, she said, "I've got some interesting advertising options to show you."

In minutes they were talking about social media and mail outs and not mentioning Nate Thayer at all. Deep, deep in her gut, though, she wondered how long she could keep it that way.

Chapter Four

Nate hadn't experienced small-town life for a long time, and while some things had definitely changed, others remained memorably the same. The Thunder Ridge Public Library was a perfect example.

Still a two-story structure with a basement and ground-level square footage, the seventy-year-old building had the same heavy wooden tables and chairs and ancient shelving Nate remembered. Still smelled the same, too—a little bit like old books and a little bit like the dogs that had always been allowed to accompany their owners indoors. The major difference as far as he could tell was the current librarian, Holliday Bailey.

Ms. Bailey looked and smelled nothing like old Mrs. Rhiner, who, as Nate recalled, had resembled George Patton and smelled faintly of cooked broccoli.

"I can place a hold on some of the books you're looking for and have them sent here through our interlibrary loan system. The problem is you're not a local, Mr. Thayer. How am I going to get you a library card?"

Holliday tapped shiny cherry fingernails on her mouse, her matching red lips pursed as she looked from the computer screen to Nate. "And you said you're staying at the inn? All by your lonesome?"

"That's right."

"Have you any friends in town, Mr. Thayer? Of the very close variety?"

"None with library cards they want to loan me, if that's what you're getting at, Ms. Bailey."

"That's exactly what I was getting at." When she shook her head, silky dark brown hair that looked like a shampoo ad brushed her shoulders. "We need to connect you with someone in a position of power...so you can get the books you need."

Nate grinned. Holliday Bailey was one of the most physically stunning women he had ever met. Long neck, perfect bone structure and slender as a willow with spitting-intelligent eyes, she would require a man who could keep up with her. While Nate was pretty sure he could, he knew instantly that the woman was harmless, far more interested in playing with his mind than with any other part of his anatomy.

"Thanks for your help."

"You're more than welcome."

Shaking his head in admiration, Nate walked away, heading for the nonfiction section and trying to remember if he'd ever dated anyone like her. His tastes had always run to women whose beauty was subtler, their attractiveness unfolding the more he got to know them.

That thought led inevitably to the woman who was trying so hard to ignore him.

When he'd first met Isabelle Lambert, he hadn't intended to be anything other than polite. She'd been a high school student, one year behind him in school, and a waitress, and he'd respected that. In his senior year of high school, Nate had taken to spending part of every day at The Pickle Jar, where he could order a drink and, when he had the extra cash, a sandwich and study for a couple of hours without being interrupted, since his friends rarely if ever showed up at the deli. Izzy had waited on him a number of times.

She seemed to be there, working or studying at the counter, anytime he came in. Hazel-green eyes and sandy-brown hair she scraped back in a nondescript ponytail wouldn't have drawn his notice necessarily, but her manner did. Calm, serious and almost deferentially polite, she was so different from the other teenage girls Nate knew that she became a puzzle to him, and he loved a good puzzle.

"You're very welcome to stay and study as long as you like," she'd told him when he'd asked if they needed the table during one lunch hour. Her eyes, free of makeup, had held his gaze steadily and all of a sudden he'd realized they were large and changed color—sometimes the color of an aspen tree's leaves, other times the color of its bark.

"I see you studying at the counter," he'd said in his first real attempt at conversation with her. "Whose classes are you in?"

He'd noticed her mouth then—pink, unglossed and bowed at the top as it formed a surprised O, as if she hadn't expected him to ask her anything not related to his lunch.

"I have Billings for history and Lankford for Literature. I'm working on an essay about *The Grapes of Wrath* and how a current depression would manifest differently from the Dust Bowl Migration of the 1930s. Especially on a local level."

He'd whistled. "Who assigned that as a topic?"

She'd hesitated a second. "No one. *The Grapes of Wrath* was assigned reading, but I chose the topic. It's interesting."

Her intelligent eyes had lowered as if she'd thought

she'd said something she shouldn't have, and he'd noticed a pulse beating rapidly at the base of her slender neck. In that moment she'd reminded him of a cross between a falcon and a hummingbird. And he'd had a surprising revelation as an eighteen-year-old, realizing that around most girls, his smiles started on the outside and sometimes worked their way in; with Isabelle Lambert, his smiles started deep inside.

He never did get around to flirting with Izzy. One day he'd found an eagle's nest while on a hike and asked if she'd like to see it. She'd said yes, and…that had been their first date, which was weird, because he hadn't planned to date anyone at all. He'd dated plenty in high school, and he hadn't wanted the distraction or the drama so close to graduation.

Because he'd known he was leaving for Chicago at the end of summer, he and Izzy had agreed to keep things light. They had broken that agreement in a dozen different ways.

"Yum! It *so* pays to have friends in the right places." Holliday's naturally sultry voice carried clearly through the library. "Mmm, lunch. And at exactly the right time. I'm wasting away."

On the heels of her exclamation came the aroma of food and a voice that responded, "I wanted to check on the availability of the Black Butte room for a class on ASL in the Workplace next week. I forgot to reserve the room, so I thought I'd bring a little lunch to butter you up."

Nate heard the crinkling of a paper bag. "Pastrami, Swiss and coleslaw on rye?" Holliday sounded reverential. "I will give you anything your heart desires."

"You're so easy."

"Is that rumor still circulating?"

Peering around the row of books, Nate let his eyes

confirm what his ears and nose already told him: Holliday's visitor was Izzy, bearing food from The Pickle Jar.

Shaking her head, Izzy admonished around a smile, "Holly, lower your voice. Don't give the gossips anything else to complain about. Last week, Evelyn Cipes was in the deli grousing that we're the only town between here and Portland with a librarian who wears stilettos to work."

"Goody! I loathe stereotypes. Want to join me in my office while I do justice to this delicious meal? I'll get Maggie to cover the front."

"Sure."

Nate sprang into action before he had time to think. "Talk about ironic." He addressed himself to the librarian as his stride carried him toward her desk. "Isabelle keeps telling me she doesn't have time to talk to me, and yet everywhere I go, there she is." He leaned forward to speak confidentially. "I think she's following me." He raised a brow, hoping the unique Ms. Bailey would play along. "Do *you* think she's following me?"

The brunette looked delighted. "I don't know," she whispered loudly. "Let's find out." She looked at her friend. "Izzy, have you been stalking this big, good-looking man?"

Izzy looked horrified. Nate would have laughed if not for the fact that he didn't feel like letting her off the hook so easily. Why the devil was she treating him like a stranger—and a very unwelcome one?

"Of course I'm not stalking. I don't stalk." Trying hard not to glance at him, she told Holliday, "I better get back to work."

"I thought you were going to have lunch with me," her friend protested.

"I know. I forgot that I need to get back. There's a big party coming in for…brisket."

"Yeah, I heard brisket is trending today." Nate leaned

casually against the desk, still addressing himself to Holliday. "I don't believe her. Do you?"

The brunette's forehead creased. In lieu of answering, she asked, "How do you know Izzy?"

One glance at Izzy's face told him she did not want him to answer.

"We knew each other in high school," he said, watching her closely.

"No kidding." Holliday looked at Izzy, whose expression gave her the appearance of someone standing in line to get a root canal. "Were you…good friends?"

Fifteen years after he'd first noticed her, Izzy still had skin like a porcelain doll. He could see the red flush beneath the creamy fairness and wondered why seeing him again was so hard for her. He hadn't returned to Thunder Ridge expecting to see her but considered their reunion a bonus. They may have been kids when they were together, but they'd shared adult experiences he still hadn't shared with anyone else. And there were questions, unanswered for fifteen years now.

"I thought we were good friends," he answered Holliday's question. "Certainly enough to merit a few minutes' worth of catching up. That's what old friends do when they meet again. Right?"

"I know *I* would." Holliday's red lips curled with humor, her heavily lashed eyes darting with rabid curiosity between Nate and Izzy, who frowned mightily at her friend.

Suddenly, the sheriff from yesterday flashed in Nate's mind. Was he the stumbling block to their spending a little time together? Nate may not have expected to see Izzy on this trip, but now that they were together, he'd like some closure. Not that he was channeling Dr. Phil, but he had questions that were fifteen years old. Didn't she? If nothing else, he'd like to know why she'd refused to be in touch with him after she'd miscarried their baby.

"Five minutes," he said to Holliday. "That's reasonable, don't you think?"

"Take ten," she suggested, ignoring Izzy's expression.

"You're right. Ten. Can we use the meeting room?" When Holliday nodded, he turned to Izzy. "One-sixth of an hour, Isabelle. My watch has a timer. I'll even let you hold it, so you'll know I'm not cheating."

Maybe he didn't know Izzy well anymore—maybe he never had—but he could see the wheels spinning in her head. She was trying to think of a way to reject his overture, again. And then—

"Ten minutes," she said decisively. "And then I have to go."

If Nate could feel the waves of curiosity rolling off Holliday, he was sure Izzy felt them, too, but she strode ahead of them toward the Black Butte room without a backward glance.

At the door to the meeting room, Izzy stopped, allowing Holliday to pass ahead of her. The librarian reached into her bra, of all places, to extract a set of small keys, one of which she used to unlock the heavy oak door. She flipped the light switch and stepped back, only slightly less provocative when she asked, "Do you need a chaperone?"

Izzy looked as if she was about to say yes.

"We'll manage," he replied. "Maybe another time." Taking Izzy's arm, he led her into the room. Holliday closed the door behind them, gently albeit reluctantly.

A rectangular table and a dozen or so chairs filled the center of the room. Framed posters of foreign countries graced the plain ivory walls.

Izzy pulled out of Nate's grasp without waiting another second. Yanking out a chair, she sat and glanced at her watch. "Ten minutes, and your time starts…now."

Exasperation poured into him. "Fine." Pulling out the chair right next to hers, he sat facing her. "Where did you go after you left town? Did you ever get that business degree you wanted so badly? What brought you back to Thunder Ridge, because from what I recall, you hated it here? And why the hell are you so angry after all these years?" Glancing at his own watch, he set the timer and said, "Okay...go."

The eyes he remembered as tender and affectionate and innocent clouded with surprise and confusion, and he wasn't above a moment of pure satisfaction as he realized he'd thrown her off guard.

Seconds ticked by without a verbal response. The expression in her eyes morphed from confusion to pain, and that was when regret slammed into him like a sledgehammer. He knew that expression—it was the one she'd worn the night she'd told him she was pregnant and again on the day he'd left for college. It mirrored the pain he had felt the day his mother had phoned from Oregon to tell him Izzy had left town with strict instructions—instructions he hadn't followed—for Nate not to get in touch with her again. She wanted, Lynette Thayer had said, "to start over...move past her mistakes...forget everything that had happened."

Was that what this was about? She'd "forgotten" everything between them, and he was bringing it up again? Maybe what happened between them was a secret she kept from the important people currently in her life. The sheriff flashed to mind again, and Nate sighed. What right did he have to make her dredge it all up if she didn't want to? None, probably. But he had something he needed to say, just to her.

"As hard as things got, I have good memories of that summer, Izzy, good feelings about the months before we became two high school kids who had to deal with some very adult decisions. I worried about you when you left without telling me." He hesitated, then figured, what the hell? He'd probably never get this chance again. "It made sense that you'd want to move on with your life. You certainly had that right. I get that. But it would have been nice to know you were okay after the miscarriage. One final check-in call." He wiped a hand down his face. "I suppose I still don't understand why we never said goodbye. So, how about we begin with my last question and work our way back? Why do you still want to avoid me?"

Miscarriage.

Izzy heard nothing after that word. *He thinks I miscarried our baby?*

Was it really possible that Nate believed there was no baby, no toddler, no child or teenager to wonder about? That he believed she'd moved on from their relationship more or less as he had—older, wiser…and childless?

Her breath came fast and shallow as the truth became clear. One thing about Nate: he didn't lie, not even when it would be more convenient. He hadn't said "I love you" to get her into bed, and he hadn't said their baby wasn't his when it would, after all, have been the word of the high school valedictorian against the girl everyone had assumed would follow in her mother's footsteps.

No, he didn't lie. But he had been lied to.

Izzy's palms grew damp as nausea filled her stomach.

"We have a time constraint here, Izzy." Irony shaded Nate's voice. "Not that *I* have anywhere pressing to be today."

He tilted his head in question. *Will you change your mind and talk awhile?* Nate was in his early thirties, like she was, but in this moment, even beneath the fluorescent glare, he looked eighteen again, sweet and teasing and persuasive.

She wanted so badly to get out of here so she could think. For the entire length of her son's life, she'd told herself that Nate knew he'd fathered a child and simply didn't care. She'd thought he'd been content to assume his child had been adopted and that he was completely off the paternal hook.

His lips curved as he gazed at her, and an electric feeling zinged through her veins. The first time she'd noticed him watching her, she'd been waiting tables at the deli, joining sweet, elderly Mr. Wittenberg in a quavering rendition of "Happy Birthday" while Mrs. Wittenberg giggled at the giant slice of New York cheesecake Izzy had set in front of her. The dessert was topped with so many candles Mrs. Wittenberg's face had glowed like a girl's in its light.

The Wittenbergs had been married as long as Izzy or anyone else could remember. They'd been old that long, too, and tended to look after each other like a parent hovering over a newborn—with a tenderness and tolerance that was both enviable and, for Izzy, as out of reach as the burning sun.

After Mrs. W had blown out her candles, with help, Izzy had headed toward the kitchen, passing the booth where Nate had been nursing an iced tea and studying. That was when she'd noticed him watching her. Holding her gaze steadily, he'd said, "That's exactly how I want to spend my birthday when I'm their age."

She'd started loving him a little bit right then. By the time she'd realized she was pregnant, Izzy had loved Nate Thayer with every fiber of her teenage heart. When it had appeared he didn't love her at all, she had taken cold comfort in believing he was just one more irresponsible, self-centered teenage boy who'd had his fun and wanted to get on with a life that did not include a girl he didn't love and a baby he hadn't intended to make. Keeping that thought always in the forefront of her mind had gone a long way toward helping her let go of Nate. It had helped her let go of romantic fantasies altogether.

But now...

Dizziness and nausea rolled through her again. "Did

your mother tell you about the miscarriage?" Was that her voice? She sounded calm.

Nate nodded.

Raw, burning anger filled Izzy's body. She started to shake.

"I know it must have been painful. Terrible," he said. "But I could never figure out why you didn't tell me yourself. You were a gutsy girl."

Gutsy. Is that what he thought? "I was never gutsy. I was always terrified." She regretted the words the moment they left her mouth.

No hint of a smile remained around his lips. "That would have been more reason to phone, wouldn't it?"

There was no miscarriage to phone about! She wanted to scream it. Shriek it. She wanted to find his parents and throttle them, and she was not a violent person.

Was she "gutsy" enough to tell him the truth now?

Would the truth have made a difference back then?

No. Nate went to college and moved on with his life. She was just the girl who was going to ruin everything for him. Her baby was such a "mistake" that Nate's parents chose to pretend he'd died rather than be part of his life.

Revulsion filled Izzy until she honestly thought she was going to throw up.

My son is not a mistake, and nobody—nobody—is going to make him feel that way. The Thayers had thrown away the chance to get to know Eli, to be part of his life, to influence him in a positive way. The Thayers—Nate included—had never done a thing to deserve Eli Lambert.

"You were involved with college, Nate."

"So?"

"You'd moved on with your life."

"I was in Chicago, not the antipodes. I cared about what was happening back here."

Which is why you found another girl right away. "You were busy all the time—"

"Not too busy to talk to you, damn it!" Obviously frustrated by her responses, Nate slammed his hand on the heavy oak table in the meeting room.

"We cannot do this here," she hissed, rising from her chair and glancing at the door as she slung her purse over her shoulder. She shook her head. "I don't want to do this at all."

"Too bad." Nate blew the air forcefully from his lungs as he, too, rose. The conference room felt claustrophobic as he advanced on her. "Look, I didn't come to town intending to stir up the past. I didn't even know you'd be in Thunder Ridge."

Izzy's teeth clenched. Was that supposed to make her feel better?

"But we're both here, for the first time since we were kids." His demeanor softened. "That's got to mean something."

Oh, no, she refused to get sentimental. Maybe he had nothing to lose by rehashing the past, but she did. Eli did.

"It means you have business in town, and I liked Thunder Ridge enough to make my home here. That's *all* it means."

"You sure?" He regarded her steadily, and her skin began to prickle with awareness. "I have time tonight. We can have dinner."

"No." Absolutely no. Scraping back her chair, she rose so quickly she got dizzy.

With one hand on the table, he leaned into her. "You're going to keep avoiding me, aren't you?" His eyes and his voice were velvet—soft, smooth, strong.

She remembered that voice in the dark, remembered the way his whisper had seemed to penetrate her very pores and how she'd often thought she could feel his words vibrate inside her.

"Meet me tonight," he stated again.

"I have a previous engagement."

"Break it."

"I can't do that." She had to go somewhere and think. Right now. Making a show of looking at her watch, she announced, "I have to go. I'm late for work."

"Fine." He straightened. She felt a momentary relief until he said, "Call me later today when you know your schedule, and we can set up a time to talk more."

Without answering, she headed toward the door.

"Don't wait too long, Izzy."

Reflexively, she turned. His blue eyes were narrowed and considering, trying to decide, she knew, if he could trust her to call him. Black hair, as thick and shiny as it ever was, fell across his tanned forehead.

Her reluctance to see him was only whetting his curiosity.

Swallowing hard, she shot out the door, realizing he'd followed right behind her when she heard someone say, "Nate Thayer, is that you?"

The voice belonged to an older man. She didn't recognize it right off and refrained from turning around. Even though she was a fixture in town today, back in high school she'd primarily hung around the deli or by herself at the library. Or in the broken-down trailer she shared with Felicia. It was Nate who'd been something of a local hero. Varsity football quarterback who'd led the Thunder Ridge Huskies to their first state finals. Valedictorian. Polite and well raised. Never made a misstep until he'd met her.

Izzy walked quickly toward the front of the library. Holliday was still at her desk, apparently postponing her lunch hour. Her customary provocative smile was in place as she looked at Izzy, but it dropped the second she noted her friend's expression.

"Do you want to talk?" she offered, half rising from her chair.

Izzy had always been a private person—more so, she had been told, than most. For once, though, she knew she needed her best friends.

"Derek's bringing pizza tonight," she managed to choke out as tears clogged her throat.

"I'll bring a salad and drinks and see you around six thirty."

The tears reached her eyes. "Thanks." Quickly scrounging in her purse, she found her sunglasses, slipped them on and gave one wave to Holliday before leaving the library.

The sun was directly above her, the clouds picture-perfect in the late-June sky as Izzy stepped onto the street. After two slogging steps toward the deli, she changed her mind and headed for home. She'd been at work since five that morning; no one would complain if she took a break, and she didn't want to see anyone now, not even Henry or Sam. For the first time in memory, she was actually glad Eli wouldn't be home when she got there.

She couldn't remember a time when she'd felt more confused. If Nate thought she'd had a miscarriage, then he wasn't the total bad guy she had believed him to be all these years. On the other hand, he'd wanted her to put their child up for adoption and left her in the dubious care of his parents while he pursued a solo life in Chicago. So, he wasn't the man she'd once hoped he was, either. Did she owe him the truth today?

Arms swinging, feet pounding the hot pavement, she wished she could outrun her thoughts.

What she needed tonight was a little pizza, a little wine, a whole lot of ice cream and her friends to remind her of who *she* was: a woman tasked with the job of protecting her son from heartache and confusion. A single mother by circumstance and by choice, committed to raising a secure, confident human being who knew he was the pride and joy of the people who loved him. The biggest threat to her success would be falling, once again, for a man who didn't want to be a husband to her or a father to their son.

Her heart couldn't handle making that mistake twice.

Chapter Five

"Wow."

Izzy smiled weakly at Derek's stunned expression. She'd felt far too nervous to take more than an obligatory bite of the pizza he had brought over, but he and Holliday had done justice to the extra-large "kitchen sink" pie while Izzy pieced together the story of her high school romance. When she got to the part where she'd told Nate she was pregnant and his parents had convinced them that having the baby would ruin their lives and their child's, Derek stopped chewing, leaned his elbows on his knees and listened intently. His brows lowered more with each word, and Holliday traded her dinner plate for a wineglass, her green eyes filling with concern.

"Were his parents pissed off?" she asked.

"They didn't show it. Not in the beginning," Izzy answered honestly. "They were certainly disappointed. I think they'd started Nate's college fund the day he was born. He was voted Most Likely to Succeed *and* prom king in his senior year of high school. All set to take the world by storm."

"Were they compassionate?"

"At first." As her mind traveled back to the memories, Izzy felt the surge of emotions she usually resisted. "The Thayers made their points kindly. That was the problem. If they'd been furious right off the bat, maybe I would have kept my perspective. And before Nate left for school, he was…"

She closed her eyes against stinging tears.

"Before he left for school, Nate was what?" Holliday urged.

"Protective. He seemed to care…about me *and* the baby. He told his parents he was worried about how I would manage if there were problems with the pregnancy and he wasn't here. He knew my mother wasn't going to be any help. Plus, choosing the adoptive parents, dealing with the lawyer—he said it would be too much for me alone." His beautiful eyes had been awash with concern. No one had ever—ever—looked at her that way before.

He'd even kissed her as he'd left for the airport. They hadn't been romantic since she'd given him the news. Pregnancy had hijacked their relationship. The goodbye kiss had been just a sweet, soft touch of his lips to her cheek, but he'd done it right in front of his parents.

"I didn't know anything about family back then. It was easy to convince myself that what Nate and the Thayers were offering was as good as it ever gets. I even began to pretend Mrs. Thayer was my mother-in-law."

"What happened when you realized you couldn't go through with the adoption?" Shifting on Izzy's sofa so that she was more comfortable, Holliday nursed her wine while she waited for more of the story.

"I worked up the courage to tell the Thayers I wanted to keep the baby and give them the gift of a wonderful grandchild. I'd honestly convinced myself they'd be happy. I said I was sure Nate would fall in love with the baby the minute he saw it."

Derek swiped a hand down his face. He knew what was coming. By her expression, so did Holliday.

"Yeah—" Izzy nodded "—that spooked them. I was an obstacle to everything they'd worked so hard for. Suddenly, they weren't as nice anymore, and I was such an idiot, I was actually surprised."

Derek swore, colorfully. "You weren't an idiot. You trusted them, and they were—"

"Frightened," she said before he could use a much less kind word. "They were really frightened. Mrs. Thayer even told me that Mr. Thayer hated being a 'glorified janitor,' but he'd had to take any job he could to support a family. She implied their marriage wasn't all that happy and asked if that was what I wanted. She said Nate had dreamed of being an architect since he was ten years old and wouldn't it hurt me to see his resentment if he stayed in Thunder Ridge and wound up like his dad."

"Powerful stuff," Holliday said quietly.

"Yes, but I didn't let that stop me. I told her I was strong and a good worker, and I would never let Nate quit college. I said I'd work as hard as I had to for as long as I had to. She looked at me for a long time, and I thought I'd actually convinced her. But then she brought out the cannon."

Derek frowned. "What do you mean?"

"She showed me a photo Nate had mailed his parents. He had his arm around a girl. They were at a party, and they were grinning at each other. She was really beautiful... stunning...wearing an evening gown, and he was in a tuxedo. They looked just the way I'd imagined us looking if we'd gone to the prom together. And Mrs. Thayer said, 'I'm sorry, Isabelle, I really am. But Nate has plans, too. Does he look like a boy who's thinking about becoming a father with the girl he dated *one summer* after high school?'" Izzy shrugged sadly. "It was the truth."

"What did you do?" Holliday set her glass on the table, tucked her legs to her chest and rested her chin on her knees as she watched Izzy.

"I told Henry and Sam I was pregnant, and they helped me move to Portland to live with a friend of theirs. My mom had done one of her disappearing acts, so no one thought it was strange that I left."

"And he just carried on with his life?" Derek looked and sounded disgusted.

"That's what I thought." She explained the rest of the story as she knew it—how she had impulsively told Mrs. Thayer she didn't want to speak to Nate ever again, and how today she'd discovered that Nate thought she'd had a miscarriage.

Holliday put both hands to her mouth.

"He should have looked for you!" Far from behaving like the levelheaded sheriff the townspeople had come to trust, Derek stormed around the room. "You were a kid, and you were alone. Now he thinks he can come back here like the prodigal son. I've seen him all over town, shaking hands like he's running for mayor. I don't know how long he plans to stay, but we are not going to make it easy for him."

Holliday lowered her hands. "Now you're talking, Wild Bill," she said. "Let's take him out to the stockade."

Derek glared. "I don't endorse a mob mentality, which you would know if you ever bothered to come to a town meeting. I'm talking about loyalty and invoking a sense of community on Izzy's behalf."

"Or we could babble him to death."

"Now look—"

"I love you two." Watching her bickering friends, Izzy felt a burst of thankfulness for them both. "But I don't want you to do anything. Maybe Nate didn't love me the way I loved him, but he was a good person at heart."

"Except when he cheated on you the first chance he got," Derek reminded her furiously. "While you were pregnant."

Yeah, except for that, which was so out of character. Izzy frowned.

"Izzy," Holliday interjected quietly, "what do *you* want?"

Nate's face, the way it had looked today in the library, lodged in Izzy's mind. He had been intense, earnest... interested? Yes, he'd looked interested in her, in the way that had always made a flight of butterflies rise and swirl inside her.

What did she want? What she had always wanted, she supposed. A white picket fence. A husband, a few kids and a dog. A yard filled with laughter, a house filled with love. And a future that seemed predictable even if it wasn't, really. She wanted all the things she'd thought would never be hers until she'd met Nate Thayer and started to believe that a future was possible.

"Come on, jump in. What are you waiting for?" Grinning, water glistening on his shoulders and dripping from his hair, Nate bobbed in the swimming pool at The Summit Lodge and challenged Izzy. "I'll race you. Winner gets a neck rub in the hot tub."

Izzy stood at the edge of the pool in the perfect light of an early summer evening and shivered. She wasn't cold—she was nervous.

Nate's father was the head of housekeeping and janitorial services at The Summit, a seventy-five-year-old lodge built of giant beams and rough stones, hundreds of which formed a fireplace and chimney so wide and deep that Santa, his sleigh and eight reindeer could have fit into it all at once. Constructed during the pre-WWII years, The

Summit nestled at the base of Thunder Ridge and had been the site of numerous movies and, in its day, celebrity weddings. Now it was a tourist destination, hosting skiers all year round. Izzy had never been here before.

Working for his father in the summers throughout high school, Nate cleaned the pool area and mopped the lobby floor at four in the morning. He was perfectly comfortable in the lodge and absolutely at home in a pool.

"Nate, I don't… I'm not really…" *Oh, just say it.* "I'm a terrible swimmer. I never learned, not really, and I…I'm kind of afraid of the water." In fact, she felt a little sick just standing at the edge of the deep end of the pool.

Surprise altered his features. Diving beneath the surface, he swam to where she stood, then emerged, looking like a merman, somehow otherworldly and more perfect than real life. Pushing himself out of the water, he stood before her.

"You sure look good in that bikini."

Izzy shivered again as his gaze embraced every bit of her body not covered by the purple triangles.

"Trust me?" he asked, and she nodded yes. Because she did. Over the past several weeks she had begun to trust Nate Thayer more than she'd ever trusted anyone.

Taking her hand, Nate walked with her to the shallow side. There was no one in the pool, save for the two of them. With snow clinging tenaciously to the side of the Ridge, most of the lodge guests were still skiing. The magic of swimming while the late-afternoon sun glistened on the water and on the snow just above the pool area was not lost on her.

"We'll take it as slow as you want." His voice was coaxing as he led her into the water, the shock of cold offset by the warmth of his hand and his eyes.

First, he held her around the waist while he taught her to trust her body to float. The delicious sensation of water slipping between their skin distracted her from fear, and eventually she didn't know what was more buoyant, her mood or her body, as she realized the water was supporting her. Their legs tangled happily as he moved them into the deeper area and taught her to tread water.

He helped her to float on her back and to feel comfortable submerging her head, every word, every gesture, gentle and encouraging. Then, when she was so relaxed she thought she could stay in the pool forever, Nate made magic. Having her hold his shoulders, her body resting on his back, he plunged them both beneath the surface, giving her the experience of swimming underwater. She felt like a mermaid! Never before had she realized that trust could feel so exhilarating or that safety in another person's care was such a gift.

When they resurfaced, she was laughing, and so was he. "You did it," he said. "You're a water baby."

"'Baby' is right." She giggled, pleased and embarrassed by his obvious pride in her. "I only did what most five-year-olds can do."

"I don't know too many five-year-olds who can swim *and* rock a bikini," he pointed out, fire in his eyes and an intoxicating huskiness in his voice. "And you are definitely, definitely doing both."

Delight filled every nook and cranny of Izzy's body.

Holding on to the side of the pool, she and Nate grinned at each other. One of his arms curved around her, his hand on her back. And then, as if the lapping water were nudging them, they moved closer until her legs rested on his hips and both his arms were around her. They weren't two bodies anymore. The water and the wonder created the illusion that they were one. Or maybe, Izzy imagined dreamily, less than one; it was as if they moved inside a single cell.

As their lips met and their chests touched, she felt Nate's heart beat with hers. *For* hers. Suddenly, she couldn't think anymore and, for once in her life, felt no need to. With every word, every action, he made her feel important, special exactly as she was.

Lingeringly, as if they had all the time in the world, they spoke by touch and in kisses—soft and sweet, warm and deep, a language that, tonight, was all theirs and theirs alone. Izzy knew that loving Nate had changed her. She would never, ever be the same again.

She would never, ever want to be.

Anticipating getting Izzy's voice mail after several rings, Nate was vacillating between leaving a message and hanging up when finally the ringing stopped, and a tired voice answered, "Hello."

Concerned momentarily that he'd woken Izzy up, he checked the digital clock by his bed in his room at the inn: eight thirty. "It's Nate. Did I wake you up?"

There was a pause. "No."

"Are you home?"

Another pause. "Yes."

"You busy?"

He thought he heard a soft sigh. "No."

He stared at the mug of coffee on his end table. Fourth cup of caffeine since he'd left her today. He was never going to sleep tonight, but he craved the taste of coffee when his mind wouldn't settle, and at the moment every one of his thoughts felt like a speeding train.

Izzy had already told him to get lost, hadn't she? *Get lost* was closure.

Problem was, he seemed not to want to let it go, and the dog-with-a-bone feeling persisted. It didn't feel half-bad. For the past couple of years, he hadn't cared enough about anything to fight his way upstream.

When Julianne, his now ex-wife, had suggested they separate, she'd said, "We have a pleasant relationship, Nate. A nice life. But there's not much passion, is there?" She'd said it gently, clearly not looking to blame, and in the end he'd had to agree. There hadn't been much passion—in or out of bed. There should have been: they were both good-looking, smart, and worked in similar fields. Somehow, though, they'd been like two matches without the friction necessary to strike a spark. He wouldn't have ended the marriage over that, however. Commitment, responsibility— those were the principles on which he based his adult life. When Julianne left, he'd tried to carry on with business as usual, but he kept getting stuck in memories. Memories of a time before his marriage, before he was truly an adult. Memories of a time when passion had been the rule rather than the exception. And not only passion in bed.

With an elbow on his knee and one hand palming his forehead, he held the phone in his other hand. "We're not finished, Izzy. You know we're not. There are things left to say."

Her response was so quiet he had to strain to hear it. "I know."

Surprise made him straighten. "You'll meet me again?"

"Do you remember Hooligan's restaurant in Trillium Springs?"

"Sure."

"I'll be there in one hour."

"All right," he agreed, and then impulsively, before he could think better of it, he asked, "Izzy, are you in a relationship with the sheriff?"

Her hesitation lasted longer than before. "No."

Good. He thought it, decided not to say it. "See you in an hour."

As he ended the call and stood, he felt a rush of anticipation in his body, the kind he hadn't felt in a long time. The kind he used to feel just before he'd leave his house and head to the diner, knowing she would be there.

Chapter Six

Hooligan's was about thirty minutes away from her home in Thunder Ridge, but after hanging up with Nate, she'd changed clothes and left her house immediately, because she'd wanted to arrive first, get a table and look as if she was calm and in charge of the situation.

She sat facing the door, an iced tea she wasn't sure she could swallow on the table in front of her.

Holliday and Derek had left before Nate phoned, and she hadn't told either of them she was meeting him. Derek would have said she was nuts; Holly would have commended her for her courage, but courage had nothing to do with why she sat at the heavily laminated wood table way in the back of the restaurant. When he'd said they weren't finished, everything inside her agreed. She wanted to see him again.

When Nate walked in, she thought she was ready, but the first sight of him made her pulse increase unsteadily and perspiration rise to the surface of her skin. His physical appearance was still powerful. A black T-shirt hugged his broad shoulders, skimmed across his still-flat belly and disappeared into pale blue denims that perfectly outlined the glorious V of a *very* fit body. He wouldn't be solid muscle unless he worked out, a fact that made her squirm a bit in her aqua sundress. Lately, other than the occasional myocardial-infarction-inducing bike ride, she'd talked herself into believing that work, housekeeping and climbing the bleachers to watch Eli's track meets provided all the exercise she needed.

As he gazed around, clearly expecting her to be seated toward the front of the restaurant, she took a more objective look at him than she'd gotten the past couple of times they'd seen each other. The impossible thickness of his black hair had been one of the first things she'd noticed when he'd started coming to the deli during his senior year of high school. Her own hair was a nondescript brown, straight and fine. Unfortunately, Eli took after her in that department. And Nate's face—it was worthy of a sculpture, with angles and lines that seemed to be a deliberate attempt on the part of Mother Nature to create something flawless. The decade and a half since his teenage years had been good to him. Or maybe he lived an easy life unlikely to leave its imprint in signs of fatigue or stress.

A passing waitress stopped to talk to him. Nate's answering smile transported Izzy to the past, when the kindness and concentration he'd shown her had made her feel special.

"Man, I was a cheap date," she said beneath her breath, in no hurry for him to notice her this evening. If she could have, she'd have sat there indefinitely, observing the man who, when still a boy, had changed her life so profoundly.

When finally he spotted her, his attention became laser sharp, and the waitress's smile fell.

Nate headed in her direction. Izzy knew she'd be lying

to herself to say she wasn't excited by his single-minded focus. The anxiety roiling in her stomach turned into a frisson of...*just admit it, Izzy*...pleasure. *Drat!*

Yeah, that's how you reacted fifteen years ago, too, and we know how that turned out.

She'd taken psychology and early-childhood development courses in community college; she knew that neglect in childhood led to a desperate search for love wherever and however one could find it. She was over that, thank you very much.

Straightening her back, she reached for her iced tea, intending to take a nonchalant sip, but got no further than her fingertips touching the moist, icy glass. Nate's expression—so focused, so intense—made her breath come shallow and fast, no matter what her brain told her.

He slipped into the booth across from her, never breaking eye contact. "Thank you."

She didn't have to ask, *For what?* His wry smile said he knew she hadn't wanted to meet him.

After an answering nod, silence stretched until the waitress arrived with a menu.

"Are you eating?" he asked Izzy.

"I already had dinner."

"So did I," he told the waitress, then deferred again to Izzy. "Dessert?"

She shook her head. "No, thank you."

He considered her, then looked at the waitress, taking note of her name tag. "Kimmy," he said. The younger woman's instantaneous smile conveyed that she thought Nate was yummier than anything on the menu, making Izzy glad she had changed out of jeans and a T-shirt, at least, for this meeting. These days her confidence came from the inside out, but she nonetheless found her toes curling self-consciously inside the flat, comfy sandals she wore. Did she even own a pair of heels anymore?

"Do you have hot-fudge sundaes?" Nate asked Kimmy.

"I make a great hot-fudge sundae," she replied, her smile promising that she did other things really well, too.

"I'm sure you do, but here's what I'd like," Nate said. "Three dishes. One with ice cream, one with hot fudge and one filled with whipped cream. Can you do that?"

Kimmy shrugged. "If you want. We put crushed toffee and a cherry on top, too. Do you want those in a bowl?"

His eyes held Izzy's as his lips curved. "Not necessary." He passed the menu to Kimmy. "And I'll take a coffee, please."

As Kimmy left to fill the order, Izzy felt heat rising to her cheeks. *He remembered.*

"It took a full month of ice-cream sundaes for me to find out that all you really wanted was the hot fudge and whipped cream." Amusement sparked in the silver-blue eyes.

Izzy's fingers played with the damp napkin beneath her iced tea. "Back in the day when I could eat anything I wanted, yeah. I'm more careful now." *More careful about everything.*

"From where I'm sitting, it looks like you could eat a bathtub full of hot fudge and whipped cream, and your figure would be just fine. You always were too hard on yourself."

His voice still sounded like silk slipping over skin.

"So. You look good," she said. "Happy. How's your life been? Did you get everything you wanted?"

His brows rose slightly. Her tone had been clipped, oddly businesslike; she could hear it and wished she didn't sound so cold, but her voice did that when she was nervous. The time was rapidly approaching when she would need to decide one way or the other whether to tell him about Eli. She needed to find out some things first.

Nate leaned forward, resting his forearms on the table,

fingers loosely linked. "Good question. In fact, I've been thinking about that a lot lately. Did I get everything I wanted when I was eighteen?" He pondered. "It's taken a while to realize that what I wanted before I met you turned out to be different from what I needed."

She looked at him quizzically.

Kimmy returned with Nate's coffee. She set down a little dish of nondairy creamers, and Izzy knew what was coming next.

Grimacing, Nate apologized. "Sorry, I should have told you before so you wouldn't have to make two trips. I like cream," he clarified. "Or milk. Whatever you've got. No rush, though. I can wait until you bring the dessert. Oh, and two spoons. Did I say that before?"

"No, but I guessed." She glanced at Izzy, the envy plain on her face.

You're too young for him, Izzy thought. *You're too young, period. Go to college, have a career and then figure out your love life.* It was the advice she gave Eli, sprinkling it on him like salt on popcorn, hoping to coat every little kernel in his brain. Kimmy walked away, dejected, but perked up when a group of twentysomething young men came in looking for a table.

Nate followed Izzy's gaze. "You think she's older than we were when we met?"

Surprised that he'd had a similar train of thought, she answered, "Yes. I hope so, anyway. She's probably closer to twenty, don't you think?"

"Hard to tell these days. Seems like people mature earlier all the time."

Finally, she felt like smiling. "Hate to break it to you, but that answer makes you sound old enough to be her father." She inwardly cursed herself for her careless verbal slip.

An answering curve quirked his lips. "Sometimes I feel old enough."

Izzy continued to fiddle with her napkin. She wanted to ask whether he had kids, but that would invite the same question in return, and she needed a lot more information before she decided what to divulge. Carefully, she responded, "So you think kids grow up too quickly these days, hmm? Have you had some experience with that?"

"Last summer, I coached a football league for a group of ten- to twelve-year-old boys who were considered 'at risk' in their schools. We spent as much time talking as scrimmaging. Most of the boys wanted girlfriends or claimed to already have one. They weren't even teenagers. I don't remember reaching that stage until high school."

"Interested in sex for the sake of sex?"

Nate's eyes narrowed. "No. Restless, confused about the future. Hungry for a connection they don't even know how to define." He nodded toward her hands. "That napkin's a goner."

Izzy looked down. The damp napkin beneath her iced tea glass had all but disintegrated beneath her nervous fingers.

Lifting her glass, Nate placed his dinner napkin beneath it. "Better?"

"Thank you." Clasping her hands, Izzy set them in her lap. If anxiety could be measured on a Richter scale, she'd be at a ten-plus by now.

"What makes you think I was interested in sex for the sake of sex when we were together?"

Uh...you never said I love you. *You didn't want me to come with you when you left. You didn't want our baby. You started dating another girl two months after you got to Chicago. Take your pick.*

"Nate, it was all so long ago. I don't know what you wanted," she said. "I was just referring to teenage boys and what they're like. Boys fall in lust, girls fall in love." Quickly she added, "Or we *think* we're in love. After a while, you realize you were looking for a feeling. Young romance—it makes you feel like you've conquered the world and all its dragons." She shook her head. "Adolescence is such a confusing time, isn't it? Hormones are raging. We're vulnerable. And we dive into something that seems wonderful and powerful and crucial to our happiness, and it isn't until later that we realize the relationship we thought was so important wasn't even real."

"You think our relationship wasn't real?" The friendliness had gone out of his eyes. "I don't want to make you relive a difficult time in your life, Isabelle, but if you think I was interested in sex only for the sake of sex when we were together, you're dead wrong."

"It was a long time ago, Nate. It doesn't matter anymore—"

"Would you stop saying that?" Catching his raised voice, he leaned forward and spoke more quietly. "It matters."

She wanted to believe him. She wanted it way too much. "I'm not saying you were insincere." She tried to make her shrug easy-breezy. "I prefer to be realistic these days, that's all." She leaned forward, too, hands flat on the table instead of fiddling nervously. "Being pregnant at seventeen was tough. But the hardest part was you and I being on such different pages when it came to what to do about it. I kept hoping for a different outcome than the one that was obvious from the start. I was living in fantasyland."

"How so?"

"It was my personal Cinderella story. In my version, the girl in rags gets pregnant, goes to the ball anyway in a gorgeous maternity gown, and her feet aren't too swollen to fit into the glass slipper. She marries the prince, they raise the baby in the castle and the kingdom is at peace. The end." She infused her smile with as much irony as she could. "Fantasyland. A nice place to visit, but you'd have to be delusional to think you could live there."

Nate's expression didn't change much, but when he spoke, his voice was so deep, so intimate that it felt briefly as if they were alone. "I should have been more careful with you. Right from the start."

"What does that mean?" she asked when he simply watched her instead of continuing.

"I wasn't interested in sex for the sake of sex, but I did want to make love to you. You were beautiful and sexy and smart and funny. Still are." He cocked his head. "Except for the 'funny' part. You seem more...staid now."

"Staid!"

"I said 'seem.' I haven't decided for sure."

She felt an angry flush creep beneath the neckline of her sleeveless dress. That hardly sounded like a compliment.

Nate grinned. "Settle down, because I have more to say. You can swear at me later." Making sure she held his gaze before he continued, he said, "I knew before we met that I was leaving for college. I wish I'd gotten to know you without having sex. I wish I'd protected you in that way, because you were different from everyone else. Inexperienced—in a good way. The world had already hurt you, and you were willing to give it another chance...with me. I don't think I ever told you how honored I was that you trusted me. I wish I'd taken better care of that trust."

Izzy's lips parted. Shock widened her eyes.

"When you realized you were pregnant, the guilt kicked me in the gut. But the fact is I was a lot guiltier about what I'd just done to our futures and to my parents' trust than about what I'd just done to you. I was young, and I was an idiot—that's my only excuse. You already know that. What you don't know is how much I regret leaving you with my parents. They're good people, and they cared about you, but I should have been here. Before they told me about the miscarriage, I'd already decided to come back and see things through with you. It doesn't change anything now, and maybe you won't believe that, but I want you to know. For whatever it's worth at this late date, I want you to know I'm sorry. And that I'd planned to come home."

Nate watched a fine sheen of perspiration cover Izzy's silky skin. Her chest rose and fell with each breath. He waited. He'd said it, finally unloaded as much of the truth as he had a right to give her. He wasn't sure what he expected as the outcome. Relief for her, perhaps, if there was any lingering resentment. Closure for himself, because now he'd seen her, spoken his piece, and it was over.

At seventeen, Izzy had been one of the least cynical people he'd ever met. And that in itself had been a miracle. Nate could still recall several details about the one time he'd met her mother, Felicia. Usually after a date Izzy would insist that he drop her off at the mouth of the dirt road leading to her home. One late night, however, he'd ignored her protests, driving instead to the front door.

Sitting in the dark, on the tiny porch of a trailer that rested on crunchy brown grass and gravel, had been Izzy's mother. As they'd pulled up, Felicia, with a beer can in hand, had stumbled down the steps and into the beam of Nate's headlights. A barely there nightgown had revealed more of her too-thin body than Nate had ever needed to see. In a haze of cigarette smoke so acrid it smelled as if she'd gone through the entire pack that night, she'd drunkenly dismissed her daughter and started flirting with Nate before he'd cut the engine. Izzy had been mortified. Nate had helped her get Felicia into the house and intended to stay to make sure Izzy would be okay, but she had begged him to leave so she could settle Felicia down and pour her into bed.

Nate knew that if he lived to a hundred, he would never forget the expression of pure shame on Izzy's face. She hadn't wanted to see him again after that, either, but he hadn't listened. Knowing where she came from had made him admire her all the more. Nate's parents had given him everything, including a generous dose of self-esteem. How did a girl with Izzy's background become a diligent student and reliable worker before the age of seventeen? How did she overcome her natural guardedness to look at someone with an innocence and a trust that was breathtaking?

Before he could say anything further, Kimmy arrived with a huge goblet of vanilla bean ice cream and two smaller bowls, one filled with hot fudge and the other with pillows of whipped cream. She set the dessert plus the milk for Nate's coffee in the middle of the table, then held up a handful of spoons. "So do you want one spoon for each bowl, or just one spoon for each of you?"

"One spoon for each of us." When the girl left, Nate looked across the table. "Tell me the truth—do you still love chocolate and whipped cream together?"

Izzy's breath was coming in rapid puffs; her cheeks were still pink as a cherry on top of a sundae. "Izzy, are you all right?" he asked.

"Everyone..." Her voice sounded strained. "Everyone likes chocolate and whipped cream."

"Not as much as you."

He held out a spoon, and after a brief hesitation, she took it, though she didn't dip into the dessert.

He used to think Izzy was as soft and sweet as the whipped cream that used to make her hum with pleasure when she ate it. But, inside, the vulnerability that had once defined her had grown teeth. He'd noticed the change almost instantly. Only now, sitting in the booth opposite him, did she seem vulnerable, almost fragile, again. The urge to touch her fell on him like a ton of bricks.

Before he could make a move, she set the spoon on the table with a clatter and pushed out of the booth. "I need to use the restroom."

He began to rise, too. "Izzy, is there something—"

"You stay." She held out a hand. "I'll be... I'll be back."

Grabbing her purse, she sped toward the ladies' room.

Nate heaved a giant sigh and sat. He looked at the dishes of ice cream and whipped cream and realized they were going to melt right where they sat. He and Izzy were not going to slide back into easy companionship. The comfort and rightness he'd felt that summer were not going to be recaptured. Maybe that feeling had not been anything more than youthfulness.

Pouring milk into his coffee, Nate stared grimly at the spreading clouds and muttered to himself. "That went well."

Chapter Seven

Fifteen splashes of cold water cooled Izzy's face, but not her brain, which felt as if it was on fire. Looking into the scratched mirror above the sink, she used one of the restroom's rough paper towels to wipe at the mascara running beneath her eyes.

In all the most complicated moments of her life, she'd taken one step at a time, just the next single, obvious step. But no step seemed obvious now, and she couldn't calm down long enough to think.

Nate had planned to come home. To her. To the baby.

Don't get carried away. He didn't say that...exactly. He just said he was coming home.

That was right. That could have meant coming home to help her through the adoption process and then leaving again.

Or it *could* have meant he'd been coming home to be a family with her and the baby. It *could* have meant he'd changed his mind.

Listen to you! He didn't say "love." He didn't say he was coming home to get married, raise a family and build a picket fence.

Maybe she should ask?

Stop!

Izzy looked in the mirror. Did she look crazy? She felt crazy. Reaching into her purse, she pulled out her cell, thinking she would call Holliday, but she got no further than staring at the face of the phone. Holliday wouldn't have the answers to her problems—the answer was in the mirror.

Raising her face to the wood-framed glass above the sink, Izzy breathed deeply to calm her racing mind.

I loved him. I loved him so damn much.

He was the first good and decent person she had ever cared about who'd cared about her, too. When the dream of being with him forever had died, the part of her that was willing to allow another person to break her heart had died, too. Now that hard, protective shell began to crack.

The important thing was Eli. She had to push aside her feelings, to get back out to the table where Nate sat, and become a detective. Would he welcome the news that he had a son? Was there anyone in his life unlikely to treat Eli with love and acceptance? How would his parents react?

Consciously, she steeled her nerves, made her muscles move. She was going to go back out there and be strong for her son. Just like before, she would get behind the wheel and start driving. She would not allow herself to fall apart until…well, she simply wouldn't fall apart.

Izzy did not walk, she *marched* back to the dining room, spine straight, shoulders squared, ready to set aside emotion in favor of intellect, discernment, common damn sense—

Oh, crikey.

Her feet faltered. Knees turned to jelly—warm, sloppy, melting to liquid jelly.

Nate was looking right at her, waiting for her, with a charming half grin pushing his lips.

When she reached the table, he stood. "No windows in the bathroom?"

"What?"

"When you left, the look on your face suggested you weren't coming back. I thought you might be planning to sneak through a window or out the back door."

"No." She slid into the booth and met his blue eyes. Those winking midnight eyes. "I don't run away." *Anymore.*

"Good to know. Have some dessert." Dipping the spoon into the chocolate sauce, he coated the bowl of the utensil, front and back, allowing the excess to drip back into the cup. Then he scooped a king-size pillow of whipped cream.

That's exactly how I used to do it.

Handing her the spoon, he sat back. Déjà vu smacked her upside the head, and nerves fluttered in her belly. Her fingers felt so shaky and clammy, she nearly dropped the spoon. "It's not polite to stare."

His smile deepened. "Never used to bother you."

Oh, it had bothered her, all right—hot and bothered her. He used to watch her eat the first bite. Every time they ordered a hot-fudge sundae at Hooligan's, he'd leaned back in the booth, his eyes at half-mast, a smile playing about the corners of his mouth, and she would blush—all over— as she tasted her concoction, exquisitely aware of him.

If she tried to eat now, she'd choke. *How high can a person's blood pressure rise anyway, before she has a stroke?*

When Izzy's phone chimed inside her purse, she grabbed it, letting her spoon clatter onto the saucer that held the cup of whipped cream. Holliday's face appeared on her cell phone screen.

Thank you. "Excuse me," she mumbled. "Hello!"

"Hi. Just wanted to see how you're doing. You looked

so vulnerable when Derek and I left." Holliday's voice was gentle with concern.

"Thanks. Wow. I completely forgot about the July Fourth band shell committee meeting."

"What?"

"Yeah. Are you sure you need me tonight?"

"Where are you?"

"I'm at Hooligan's with an old friend from high school."

"You're with Nate?" Holly's voice rose.

"That's right."

"Holy kamoly. And you want to leave?"

"Right, right. Well, I suppose I can still make it if you absolutely have to have details about the food booth tonight."

"Oh, yes. I *must* have details tonight," Holliday confirmed. "Not about the food, though."

"Obviously. Okay, I'll leave here in a few minutes."

"Call me when you get home."

"Will do. Bye." Izzy ended the call and arranged her features in what she hoped was an apologetic grimace. "Sorry. I've got to go. Committee meeting. I completely forgot." Oh, man. Her relationship with Nate was turning her into the town Pinocchio.

Nate's head tilted speculatively, his smile gone. "No problem."

His lips barely moved, and guilt stabbed her. She needed to see him again, to ask important questions before she decided if, when and how to tell him about Eli. But first she needed to regroup. *Right. I am not running away. I am regrouping.*

"Well, thanks," she said, already sliding across the booth. Talking to Holliday would help. Holliday, after all, had a *lot* more experience with men, even if she'd never been in exactly Izzy's situation. "Thanks for dessert and... everything."

Nate gave her a brief nod, that was all, but he rose politely. After an awkward moment—Handshake? Hug?—Izzy stupidly patted his arm and started walking. She felt his eyes on her back until Hooligan's heavy oak door closed behind her.

She didn't wait to get home to phone Holliday. Switching to her headset, she made the call and pointed her car toward home. Holly answered instantly.

"Nate was coming back. Before his parents told him I'd miscarried, he'd planned to come home from college." The words spilled out like the tears suddenly running down Izzy's cheeks. Her friend inhaled sharply. "And that's not all. He bought me ice cream tonight, and I got déjà vu, and I don't think—" She gulped. "I don't know if I ever really stopped l-l-lov—" The tears began to pour in earnest.

"It's okay," Holliday soothed quietly as Izzy became unable to speak. "I get it. I get it."

When Izzy left Hooligan's, it had not occurred to Nate that they would be together the next afternoon, watching a placid stretch of Long River, tracking the progress of kayakers and tourists on bikes as they navigated the trail along the water.

"I was surprised when you phoned," Nate said, trying not to stare at Izzy, who had donned pale blue shorts, a deeper blue tank top and a sheer, patterned overshirt for this, their second deliberate get-together. She looked utterly casual and sexy as hell. Her hair was loose, falling below her shoulders in the straight, silky curtain he remembered. "When you left the way you did last night, I wondered if I would see you again at all."

"Sorry." She glanced at him, seeming shy and…something else. "I was caught off guard last night," she admitted. "Especially when you said you'd decided to come back home. It was a surprise."

He nodded. "It was frustrating not to know where you went or how to get in touch with you. I'm not blaming," he hastened to add. "Just saying."

Izzy began to fidget, ducking her head and fingering the ends of her silky hair. She'd always been a fidgeter.

In flat sandals with multicolored straps, she looked seventeen again. "You haven't changed."

She snorted. "I've changed a lot. Anyway, that's not really a compliment unless a woman is over thirty-five. Before then, we want to change, and we want it to show."

"Interesting. I'll try to remember that." A breeze swept the warmth of the sun off their faces as they walked. "You do look the same, though. Except for your eyes. They were always intense, but back then they were unsophisticated, too—in a good way."

Today, the giant hazel eyes he'd always loved were hidden by sunglasses as her head snapped to him. "Seriously? You think you can tell a woman she's unsophisticated in a *good* way?"

"Yes, I do. You were innocent. Trusting. And with everything you'd been through..." Nate looked at her, stating the truth. "I was impressed by that."

The lower part of her face was a mask of neutrality.

"How are your parents, Nate?" she asked, changing the subject.

"I don't know if you remember that my parents had me when they were older—in their forties. By the time I was in high school, Dad had diabetes and high blood pressure. He had a heart attack in the middle of my freshman year at UI Chicago. He never completely recovered and needed a lot of help. My mom was really protective of him, but it was more than she could handle, particularly since they lived pretty far from town. I didn't think she could take care of him on her own and work, too, so I convinced them to move out. We muddled through together until I began my career and could contribute more financially."

"How is your dad now?"

"He passed a couple of years ago."

"I'm sorry. I had no idea."

"Why would you?" Putting his hands in his pockets, he mused, "Dad loved Illinois, said it felt like home. I'm glad of that."

Izzy nodded but seemed distracted. They walked in silence for a time, listening to the sound of oars lapping the water and a family's laughter.

"And your mother?" she asked finally. "Is she well?"

"Pretty much, yeah. After Dad died, she moved to a senior cooperative housing project. Keeps busy volunteering now, but I see her aging." His lips quirked. "She laments the fact that I haven't had kids."

His offhand comment seemed to snap Izzy to full attention. "Is that so."

"In fact, she's the one who convinced me to take the job that's brought me back to Thunder Ridge."

Izzy stopped walking. "What do you mean?"

He looked at the girl he'd never been able to forget, soaked in the furrow of her brow and the way wisps of her hair were carried by the breeze. "Sometimes you have to take a big step back in order to move forward," he commented quietly. "That's what she told me. She said she had a sixth sense that I needed to 'go home.' I thought it was strange, because she's not usually philosophical, and in all the years we'd been away, she'd never once referred to Thunder Ridge as home." He hoped Izzy believed him when he said, "I'm glad she pushed me to take the job. Glad I'm here again." He refrained from adding *because of you*, but that was the truth. What he knew about her life today wouldn't fit inside a thimble, but something inside him was hoping there was room for him.

Lowering her head, Izzy moved to the railing that lined their path and stared out at the water. "Did either of your parents ever come back to Thunder Ridge? For a visit, or…anything?"

Joining her, resting his elbows on the top wooden rail, he shook his head. "Uh-uh. When we were here, we lived on the farm Dad managed on top of his job at the lodge. The housing was free, and some of the furniture belonged to the landlord. There wasn't much to take with them, and my parents were both east coasters to begin with. No family to come back to in Oregon."

"I remember the farm," she said. "In fact, I remember that your father took the job there, because with no rent or mortgage your parents were able to put more money toward your college fund."

"Which they'd started the day I built an apartment building out of blocks in kindergarten." His lips twisted wryly.

"And you cried, because the teacher wouldn't let you glue it together so that it wouldn't fall down in the event of an earthquake or some other natural disaster in the classroom."

Nate slid his sunglasses down the bridge of his nose. "I told you that? Doesn't seem like a great date topic."

"I probably would have been impressed, but no, you didn't mention it. Your parents told me." Her attention shifted to the river again, where a young girl was learning to paddleboard. "I think they were reminding me that your future was planned—and invested in—a long time before you and I met. So it wasn't fair to expect you to drop all that when I got 'in trouble.'"

The beautiful day grew shadows. Anecdotes about his childhood interests and his parents' single-minded commitment suddenly seemed indulgent.

Reaching for her arm, he turned her to face him. "You

didn't get pregnant alone." He still remembered when she'd told him that. "You were right the day you said that. You shouldn't have been the only one whose plans changed. I should have stayed with you to face high school, work, the adoption lawyer, all of it. My parents should have expected that of me. I would, if I had a kid in the same situation. I understand what they were thinking at the time, what they were afraid of, but they were wrong."

She looked at him, her deeper thoughts still hidden by the dark glasses. Izzy's lips formed a perfect bow, but they looked tense.

With calls of "On your left!" a group of cyclists clattered over the wooden footbridge on which they stood. Butterflies swooped and floated in the wildflowers that lined the path. Izzy pulled away from him and started walking again. A couple with a dog crossed in front of them, and Nate dodged around, catching up with Izzy at an overlook, where a few people stood with fishing poles.

"You were seven when you read *Famous Buildings of Frank Lloyd Wright*," she said without looking at him. "At eight, you requested *The Future Architect's Handbook* for Christmas. You loved sports, but you never let your grades fall because of them, and you were one of the few teens who truly seemed to enjoy giving volunteer hours to the community."

He shook his head in disgust. "That sounds like a perfect person. And I was not."

"No. But in your parents' eyes, you were as close as you could possibly get." Her tone was tolerant, not judgmental. "Everyone deserves someone who sees him that way."

"Or who sees him realistically, recognizes his screwups and calls him on them. Izzy, don't whitewash what you went through because of us."

She did look at him then and, even with her sunglasses in place, he could see a steely strength she had not possessed at seventeen. "I'm not whitewashing anything, believe me. But if my child had a great future and I thought someone or something might take that away, I would protect him, too. A bulldozer would have to go through me to get to him. I might even make big mistakes, costly mistakes, while I tried to figure out what to do."

The vague feeling that had dogged Nate forever began to take a shape. Izzy understood passion. Despite a background that had given her no experience with loyalty, she spoke of being protective with a fierceness that humbled him to the point of discomfort.

He knew the answer to his next question but asked it anyway. Almost as if he were punishing himself. "You needed support when you had the miscarriage. I'm guessing Felicia was unavailable?"

"Felicia was never available." Izzy started walking. "When was the last time you went kayaking?" she asked, abruptly changing the subject.

"Are you and the sheriff seeing each other?"

Her head whipped toward him. "What?"

"The summer you and I dated. That's the last time I went kayaking."

"Oh." They walked a bit more. "We're friends," she muttered.

"You and the sheriff?"

Izzy nodded.

"Is there anyone else who might get his nose out of joint if he saw you in a kayak with me?"

She tilted her head, and he liked the way her hair swung in a shiny curtain around her shoulders. "Are you talking about going kayaking today?"

"That's the idea. Are you married? Engaged? Dating?"

"No, but—"

"Good. Let's go." He headed toward the rental dock.

"Wait." When he turned back, she was shaking her head. "I don't want to."

Nate sighed heavily. "Oh, that's right. You need a lot of lead-in time."

"Pardon me?"

"You weren't spontaneous. I forgot about that."

Openmouthed, she stomped toward him. "Is that a joke? If anything, I was too spontaneous with you."

Pretending to mull that over, Nate returned to the railing overlooking the river. The memory of being on the river with Izzy became vivid. When was the last time he'd felt that free, content to do nothing more than float and think about the girl in front of him? The strange, restless yearning that had prompted him to accept the job in Oregon rose inside him again.

"Sure do miss the river," he mused.

"You live in Chicago. What's that thing called that runs through your city? Oh, yeah, the Chicago *River*."

"True, we have a river. It's not the same, though. There's nothing like a hometown tributary." The grin he shot her was laced with humor. He shrugged. "Anyway, I work a lot. It's hard to relax. A vacation seems like the perfect time to get back to kayaking."

"I thought you were in Thunder Ridge on business."

He looked at her steadily. "So did I. But that was before I knew *you* lived in Thunder Ridge again."

Her lips parted ever so slightly in surprise, and he caught the swift intake of breath before she looked away from him. He had to rein in his impatience while he waited for her to say something. When she relented, her voice was low, almost flat. "Are *you* married? Or engaged?"

"No." He turned and began to walk slowly toward the rental dock. When she followed—also slowly—the intensity of his relief and pleasure came as a surprise. They were halfway there, a stack of kayaks in sight, when he added, "Not dating anyone, either. In case you were wondering."

"I wasn't."

Her expression told him she was lying. Nate turned away as a grin spread across his face.

Chapter Eight

Liar.

Heck yes, she wondered if he was dating someone.

But only because of Eli.

Mostly because of Eli.

In large measure because of Eli. She had to make sure no one was going to cause friction and unhappiness in her son's life if she told Nate the truth.

When she told Nate the truth. She was certain now that it was the right thing to do. Maybe she wasn't positive she could trust everyone in Nate's life with Eli's well-being, but she was sure she could trust Nate. And that was saying something.

As Izzy buckled the straps of the life preserver the kayak rental guy had handed her, she thought, *I'm not going to tell Nate right this second, so why am I doing this? I should be at work, coating my ulcer with a cheese Danish.*

She already had the salient information she'd hoped to attain today.

She was sorry about Nate's father and shocked that his mother had told him to come home to Thunder Ridge, knowing Izzy might be here. She didn't know about Eli, but perhaps the woman regretted her lie about the miscarriage? Izzy had never borne the Thayers any ill will, and now she believed she could forgive them altogether. That alone was a giant relief. After all, when it came to fudging on big truths, who was she to call the kettle black? Still, Izzy was just as bearish about Eli's well-being as they had been about Nate's. If Mrs. Thayer wanted to be a grandparent to Eli, she was darn well going to have to be grateful for him. Just as he was. And with Izzy as his mother.

"You doing okay over there, Gilligan?"

Nate's question made Izzy jump so hard she nearly fell into the river.

Gilligan. Oh, my Lord. She'd forgotten. She'd totally forgotten. Another feeling of déjà vu washed over her, so powerful she felt like passing out.

"Fine. I'm fine!" she lied.

Back in her kayaking days with Nate, they'd gotten caught in a sudden storm after paddling far from the more populated stretches of quiet water. Spying a finger of land, they'd pulled their tandem kayak up onto the bank, found a copse of trees to huddle beneath while they waited out the weather and sang the theme song from *Gilligan's Island*, a show they had both watched in reruns as children. On that day, during the storm, for every bar of the song they'd remembered, they'd kissed…

"Ready to get in?"

"Um…sure."

She must have had the subconscious Freudian brain fart of the century when she'd started using the nicknames Skipper and First Mate with Eli. She'd bought all the DVDs of *Gilligan's Island* to watch with him, because it had been one of the few really lighthearted memories of her childhood.

While the rental dude stood by, holding their oars, Nate stepped over to her and reached for her hand to help her in. He'd requested a tandem kayak, just like the one they'd used years before.

As soon as his hand closed around hers, a jolt of primal awareness vibrated inside her, starting low in her belly and racing down her legs.

Getting into the kayak, she held on to the dock, helping to steady the boat while Nate got in behind her. They took their oars and pushed off.

"You feeling energetic?" Nate's resonant voice made the hair on the back of her neck prickle.

She nodded.

They dipped their oars into the river and paddled in unison, finding their rhythm with unconscious ease.

The first time she'd taken Eli kayaking, he'd fallen in love with it. Even though she didn't find the time to get on the river much lately, her son was a river rat.

She and Holliday had decided that info about Nate's parents and his significant-other status was all she reasonably needed to know before she told Nate he was a father. There was nothing to stop her now.

Nothing except terror. Once she told him, everything would change.

Her relationship with Eli would change.

She dug her oar into the water. What if Eli was furious with her for not telling him about Nate sooner? Much sooner. Some kids never forgave their parents for keeping secrets. And Nate must earn more money in an hour than she earned in a day. In two days. With the deli in the red, she knew Henry and Sam were overpaying her as it was, and she was tightening her purse strings so she could take a voluntary cut in pay until business improved. *Which it would.* But until then, she and Eli were on a necessities-only budget. Nate, on the other hand, could afford the kinds of things a teenage boy coveted. What if Eli decided he wanted to live with his father in Chicago? What if Nate turned into an overindulgent parent who spoiled Eli rotten and turned her beautiful son into a shallow money-and-status-driven—

"It's not a race, Gilligan!" Nate called up to her, humor edging his voice. "Take it easy."

She didn't want to take it easy. Paddling with all her might had kept her moving forward up to this point in her life. If she slowed down, fear would capsize her.

Digging her oar into the green Long River, she couldn't paddle fast enough to outrun her imagination. How would Nate handle Eli's hearing impairment? Often, people who didn't know Eli well had trouble understanding him.

Her chest squeezed so hard she couldn't take a breath. She wanted to turn this rig around and hide under her duvet until Nate left Thunder Ridge, as ignorant of Eli's existence as when he'd arrived.

Becoming a mother had brought out all the courage in her. And all the fear, too.

Perspiration trickled down from Izzy's forehead, mingling with tears that stung her eyes, and she was glad for the physical release of paddling, as well as for the relative silence. With her emotions in her throat, she didn't want to talk.

They paddled until the picnickers and sunbathers along the river's edge faded into the background behind them and the water narrowed to a snaking channel with reeds and tree-lined banks.

As it became harder to paddle, Izzy noticed the kayak pulling toward the marshy area near the shore. She waited for Nate to lean the kayak, but it continued to drift starboard.

"Nate, we're going the wrong way. We're going to get stuck!" She paddled harder, to no avail. "Why can't we move this thing? Why—" She turned to look at him. "What…what are you doing?"

Nate's arms were crossed behind his head, his oar resting uselessly in front of him. Face turned toward the sun and glinting off his aviator glasses, he wore the satisfied smile of someone utterly at peace. Didn't he realize—

"We're going to run aground! What's the matter with you? Paddle, damn it, paddle!"

His grin reminded her of a slow dance—nice and easy. "You're still a type A rower." He clucked his tongue. "Relax, Izzy. Trust the river. The current will take you where you want to go."

Was he crazy? Cattails and saw grass clogged the river closer to the bank. "Kayaks wouldn't come with oars if we weren't supposed to paddle," she pointed out.

White teeth flashed as his laughter rang across the river. Now she remembered. This was how it used to be: Nate would be relaxed and calm. He'd be enjoying life while she worried enough for ten people. He'd make decisions and move forward while she fretted and stewed and redecided. How could she trust Eli's well-being to a man who thought so differently than she? She'd be on a Xanax drip while he took the path of least resistance. He was so…so… He was…

He was so right.

Correcting course on its own, the kayak began to float back toward the middle of the river.

Still leaning back, Nate said, "You know, I don't think you ever stopped paddling before. Good for you."

Izzy whipped around to face front again. A soothing breeze fanned her skin and ruffled the tree leaves—the only sound to interrupt the gorgeous quiet. Despite her surroundings, she felt hot and agitated.

Play it cool today. You're on a fact-finding mission, that's all. No drama. No recriminations and no big revelations. Don't show your emotions at all. Holliday had coached her before she'd left for this meeting with Nate.

But, really, who did he think he was, telling her to follow the river. To "trust the current"? All her life she'd felt like a salmon swimming upstream and never more so than when she'd realized the boy she'd thought she'd loved with all her heart did not love her. Never had she felt less capable of trusting life than when she'd been a pregnant high school senior, desperate to keep her baby *and* get an education, and give both herself and her child a decent life.

Think like Holliday. Holliday would be sarcastic or crack a joke. Holliday would tell him to *piss off.*

"You okay up there, Gilligan?"

"Piss off!" Instantly, tears sprang to Izzy's eyes and—*drat it!*—a sob caught in her throat. She had never, ever said that to anyone before. Not even in sign language.

"What's the matter?"

She paddled harder. If she couldn't stem her tears, she could pass them off as sweat.

"Whoa, Izzy, you're going to give yourself a heart attack. Slow down."

Nate increased his efforts also, which consequently reduced hers, and Izzy realized how tired she was.

"See that inlet about thirty feet up ahead? Head there, and we'll rest on land."

His tone told her not to argue, but ultimately it was her own fatigue—emotional and physical—that persuaded her. She couldn't fight it as he paddled backward directing them toward the shore. The second they reached the riverbank, however, she struggled out of the kayak, wordlessly helping to drag the boat to higher ground, then stalking toward the woods.

"Izzy, wait!" Catching up, he grabbed her arm. "Would you tell me what's wrong?"

"Just drop it."

"Not a chance. Talk to me." His eyes looked fierce.

"Okay, you want to know what's wrong? You. You're what's wrong!" Breathing heavily, she felt years' worth of fear and exhaustion and hurt boil over. "You think you can come back and tell me you're sorry you left town and, golly, you sure meant to come back, so that means you and I are at ground zero again. Well, it doesn't work that way."

"I never said that. I—"

"You don't have to *say* it, Nate. You've always gotten what you want. Good-looking, good grades, good family. Well, good for you. 'Just trust the current, Izzy.'" She threw his words back at him. "Maybe the current takes you where you want to go, but in my life, I have to row."

They stared at each other, and the awareness in his eyes told her that, for the first time, he realized how deep her resentment went. She hadn't even realized it herself until this moment.

"When did I become your enemy?" he asked.

He seemed to genuinely want to know.

Don't say anything, don't say anything...do not say anything. Remember what Holliday told you—now is not the time to get emotional.

"Never mind." She shook her head. "Forget it. Let's go back." She turned.

Nate grabbed her arm. "No. Izzy, I'm not just here because of work or for a vacation. I came back because nothing in my life, *nothing*, has ever felt as right as that summer we were together. It was special. *You* were special."

Tears leaked out the corner of her eyes, and her nose began to run. Hastily, she wiped her face, glancing toward the forest to gauge whether she could make a run for it. Nate had always been the one person who could break her heart wide-open and then make it knit shut again, tighter and harder to crack than before.

"I was 'special'? Nothing felt as 'right' as that summer?" She nodded broadly. "Wow, that is a happy surprise. There's just one thing I don't understand." *Don't do it, Izzy, don't. Holly was right—don't get emotional.* "How were you able to date another girl so soon after you left town? I don't think I could have done it if I'd been in your shoes. I wouldn't have forgotten someone so special that my entire summer felt 'right' just because we were together, and then be able to go off and date somebody else. Then again—" *No, seriously, stop yourself.* "It's also hard to understand why—if I really was that special—you never wanted to introduce me to your cool high school crowd or to your parents. At least not until I got pregnant, and you panicked and told them about me so they could convince me not to keep the baby!" Her whole body felt like a volcano ready to erupt. She marched so close she could see the dark blue rim of his eyes. "You didn't fight for *us*, you fought for your future. You knew I didn't fit into that future. And I knew it, too, I really did, but I was willing to pretend, because I—" *No. No-no-no-no-no.* "I...I—" *I forbid you to say it! If you say it, you will never be able to take it back.*

"Izzy—" he began when she halted. "Back up. What do you mean, I got another girlfriend after I left?" He scowled. "Dating was the last thing on my mind when I left town."

"I don't care if you dated." *Not much.* The photo of him and the beautiful, sophisticated blonde had been a knife in her heart. "I'm sure there were plenty of appropriate girls in Chicago."

"Appropriate?"

"Women who would have made your parents comfortable."

"Izzy, my parents were middle class with middle-class values they embraced."

"They didn't want *you* to embrace them, though."

Sighing, he rubbed his eyes. "Maybe not. But after what happened with us, I needed a break to figure things out. Post-traumatic relationship disorder." His smile was sad and ironic. "That's what a friend of mine called it."

"You're saying you had post-traumatic relationship disorder? *You* did." She looked at him in disbelief.

"Yes," he confirmed. "Hell, Izzy, do you think I didn't care that I got you pregnant? That it wasn't eating away at me that I made your life harder when it was already tough enough? Is that why you left without even calling me?" His eyes narrowed. "The baby you miscarried was mine, too."

There was no miscarriage! She nearly screamed it, but another thought intervened. "A baby you didn't want to raise in the first place? You must have been at least a little relieved to hear there was no baby."

The storm that crossed his face seemed to turn the entire afternoon dark and dangerous. "If that's what you believe, then you don't know me. You don't know me at all. Even worse, I apparently didn't know you."

He waited, staring, glaring at her, but she remained stubbornly mute. Her mind, however, was busy.

Was it possible that Nate was telling the truth about not dating and that his mother had misrepresented the situation to her, just as she'd skewed the facts when relaying them to Nate? All Izzy knew for sure from that photo was that Nate had attended some kind of formal event and posed for a snapshot with a pretty girl. If he hadn't been dating anyone else—

It doesn't matter. He didn't want to raise a baby. He didn't want a family. And you did. There was no future. Now, ironically, they had come full circle: intuitively she knew that when she told him about Eli, their complicated relationship would have to be put aside to address their son's needs.

While her brain spun a tangled web, Nate, it appeared, had had enough.

"Fine," he said between gritted teeth. Stalking around her, he headed for the kayak. "Let's get back."

Chapter Nine

"George Eliot's *The Mill on the Floss*, 1860 first edition. Oh. My. Gosh. Your wife had fabulous taste in books, Henry." Reverently, Holliday stroked the brown cloth cover of the small volume she had plucked from the cramped bookshelves in Henry Bernstein's living room. "*Northanger Abbey*, circa 1930," she murmured, reading more of the titles. "*Buddenbrooks*—another first edition. Be still, my heart." She turned toward the man seated on the couch. "Are you sure you want to donate these to the library? You have some really coveted editions here, and they're all in good condition. You could get a pretty penny."

Seated on the carpeted floor as she rummaged through a box of china she'd brought up from the basement, Izzy watched Henry nod and wasn't surprised when he said, "Elaine loved the library. She was one of its best customers. With her books displayed in a case, a little part of her will always be there, watching over everything."

Though she'd never met Elaine, Izzy had heard enough

about her through the years to feel as if she'd known Henry's wife. It was obvious that her passing had not ended their relationship.

Holliday shook her head slowly, hugging *The Mill on the Floss* to her chest. "That's lovely. Whenever you've talked about Elaine, it's obvious how much you two loved each other."

Izzy's head popped up. The indulgent, wishful tone sounded nothing like her friend. Holliday was perhaps the least romantic person Izzy knew. That was one of the things Izzy liked best about her. Holliday had lived exclusively in large cities and had traveled the world before settling in Thunder Ridge. She said she took Mae West and Diane Keaton as her role models.

Henry's hands were folded over his little tummy. His soft brown eyes smiled. "It was a good marriage. Forty years. I was a child groom, of course." He winked.

Holliday laughed, then said, "Tell us your secret for staying in love."

Izzy nearly dropped the antique chocolate pot she was unwrapping. She wasn't sure she wanted to hear this conversation today.

Swimming in a sea of uncomfortable emotions since their silent paddle back to the kayak rental place, she'd been popping antacids since last night. Last month, Henry and Sam had announced they wanted to participate in the annual Thunder Ridge yard sale. Izzy had tapped Holliday and planned to spend several hours this weekend sorting and pricing the belongings with which they were ready to part. After a sleepless night, she'd hoped that helping the brothers would distract her, but so far, no such luck.

"Lemonade and cinnamon *mandelbrodt*," Sam announced, entering the room before Henry could respond. He balanced a tray laden with four glasses of iced lemonade and a plate of the wedge-shaped cookies he baked once a week.

Jumping up, Izzy took the tray, setting it on the coffee table while Sam lowered himself to the couch beside his brother. "What were you talking about?" he asked.

"Who wants a lemonade?" she countered, hoping to derail the topic. No such luck.

"Did I hear someone say 'love'?" Sam looked as eager as a puppy with a rawhide.

It was no secret that keeping track of romances both local and global was Sam's favorite pastime. At age seventy-five, he had never married, but he had fallen madly in love at age nineteen with a girl he'd met while serving a stint in the navy. The relationship hadn't worked out, but Sam had never forgotten her and remained convinced that she was his soul mate. Every time he brought up the fact that he had lost his one true love—and he brought it up fairly often—Izzy got an uncomfortable squeeze in her stomach.

"I was asking Henry to tell us how he managed to stay in a relationship for forty years," Holliday said, accepting the glass of lemonade Izzy handed her but missing—or ignoring—Izzy's pleading stare.

She'd told Holliday all about her meeting with Nate. Confusion, anger, guilt and a pervasive sadness she could identify only as grief had dogged her since yesterday afternoon. So much so that she felt as if she had an emotional hangover today.

"True love," Sam said in answer to Holliday's query. "That's how you stay together. You find your one true love, and you never leave and you never give up." Sam considered himself an expert about relationships. "Isn't that right, Hank?" he deferred to his brother.

"That's a good start, Sammy, a good start. But, no, I don't think that's what sustains you for forty years. The question was wrong."

"What do you mean? My question was wrong?" Holliday asked.

Henry nodded. "I'm afraid so. You're assuming Elaine and I stayed in love for forty years."

Holliday, Izzy and even Sam stared at Henry in surprise.

"What are you talking about?" Sam looked horrified. "You and Elaine were *bashert*."

"What?" Still holding Elaine's book, Holliday walked over and sat in one of the chairs opposite the couch. "What does that word mean? Besh…what?"

"Bashert," Izzy murmured. She'd heard the Yiddish word often enough since coming to work for the brothers. "It means 'meant to be.'"

Sam nodded. "And you only get one. One *bashert* per customer."

"So you think we're fated to meet that one right person, or not?" Holliday seemed truly interested. That same question had plagued Izzy for years until she'd decided that true love was either a myth or something that struck rarely, like lightning.

Sam, however, nodded decisively. "That's exactly what it is. Destiny."

Reaching across the sofa cushions, Henry patted his brother's knobby hand, a gesture so sweet that Izzy felt her eyes sting. "Maybe not exactly," Henry said, a gentle curve to his lips. "The way you put it, Holliday—to meet one right person or not—implies a certain fatalism. The meeting will or will not happen despite anything we do. And if we meet our fated one, we will be together and stay together, also despite anything we do or do not do. But to be a *bashert* is not so easy, I'm afraid."

Leaning forward, he picked up a glass of lemonade and a *mandelbrodt* and took a bite of the cookie. Nodding as he chewed, he winked at his brother. "Your best batch yet." Henry issued the same compliment every time and seemed to mean it.

"So, a *bashert*," he continued, "depends on the philosophy that before our lives begin, we are given certain abilities and a mission that only we can fulfill in this world. As a gift, we are given a special person, a partnership to help us become the best 'us' we can be. But it's difficult, this business of being someone's *bashert*, because as another gift, we're given free will." With the hand holding the lemonade glass, he gestured. "Izzy knows this."

Izzy's heart began to thump hard and fast. Surely, he wasn't talking about—

"I'm quite certain she considers that Eli was meant to be her son. That she and only she was meant to be his mother."

Her heart calmed down.

"But it was her choice to have this *bashert* son of hers," Henry said. "And it is a choice to raise him, to love him through good times and less good ones. To believe so much in this special partnership that she keeps going... kept going even when he was twelve and—" he bobbed his head from side to side "—maybe not so lovable all the time. But Izzy made a choice, an agreement to stay in the mother-son relationship, because she believes in it. Being someone's meant-to-be takes great patience and perseverance. To be a witness for another's life is a sacred trust. It's easier, I assume, to maintain this commitment with one's child than with a spouse."

"But you did it?" Holliday's expression and the hesitancy in her voice mirrored Izzy's reaction. Was Henry saying that he and Elaine were not the love affair everyone had assumed? "You maintained the commitment?"

"Elaine was my witness for as long as she was alive. I was hers. Sometimes we loved what we saw, sometimes—" he shook his head "—no. But it didn't matter. We made an agreement. We kept going."

"Sounds like a lot of work," Holliday muttered.

"Finding your *bashert* doesn't necessarily make life easier," Henry agreed. "It makes it better. The next question I see in your eyes, dear Holliday, is whether we kept loving each other, and the answer to that is yes. When we looked for the love, we found it. Over and over. In forty years, we lost it many times and found it again." His eyes filled with a wistful expression that made him appear years younger. "Always better than it was before. One day of marriage to Elaine was better than a lifetime of looking for happiness someplace else."

The room went so silent Izzy could hear the others breathing. Henry and Sam were each immersed in their own memories, and Holliday quietly rose to resume her study of the bookshelves.

Izzy reached into the box of china again, but her hands shook. The newspaper-wrapped cups and saucers actually seemed to be moving, swirling together as if they were being tumbled in a dryer. She was so, so dizzy. Her heart beat so hard and so quickly, she began to fear she was having a heart attack.

I have to go. I have to go.

"Where?"

Holliday's question made Izzy realize she'd spoken out loud. Holly's eyes were huge as she stared at Izzy in concern.

"What's wrong? Do you feel sick? You look gray."

What *was* wrong with her? She felt as if she needed to run—right now and very fast. One word thrummed through her mind: *escape.*

"I need to get some air. I just… I'll be right back." Pushing to her feet, she moved as steadily as she could toward the door.

The night Nate had insisted on driving Izzy right up to her door was the night she had known they would never last.

Now, standing in front of the decrepit trailer she had

called home until she was seventeen, Izzy took several deep breaths. It had finally occurred to her that she'd been having a panic attack at Henry and Sam's earlier in the day.

For the past several years, she'd addressed fear by reminding herself how far she had come in her life. Nowhere was that more clear than amid the morass of dry weeds, rusted metal and dark memories that comprised her childhood home.

She'd once believed she was no better than where she'd come from.

The day after he'd met her mother for the first time and had witnessed the way Izzy lived, Nate had come to the deli to see her. Certain he was going to break up with her, she had prepared a goodbye speech of her own, thinking that if she beat him to the punch, there would be less chance of breaking down completely.

When Nate heard her stilted goodbye monologue, delivered in the alley behind the restaurant, he hadn't exhibited a bit of surprise. He'd simply listened, then told her he'd arranged with Henry and Sam for her to take off early. Despite her insistence that they were officially broken up, he'd persuaded her to get in his truck and had taken her to Trillium Lake, where he'd already set up a cloth-covered folding table and chairs, candles and actual china, which, it had turned out, he'd borrowed from his mother's wedding set without asking. He'd set up a CD player, tucked flowers into the needles of a pine tree and made the whole scene look magical.

"Why did you do this?" she'd asked.

He'd held her face in his hands and had said, "Because you shouldn't have to ask why when someone does something special for you." His voice had dropped to a whisper, his face moving so close to hers she could no longer see his lips. "You should understand—" he'd kissed her, and her bones had begun to melt "—that it's because *you're* special."

A decade and a half later, Izzy forced herself to walk to the front door of the broken trailer she used to call home. "Come on, Latke."

Looking like linen that refused to iron out, the Shar-Pei hauled herself up from where she'd plopped down the moment they'd arrived and followed her mommy to the cock-eyed aluminum steps. Izzy stopped there. Close enough.

Felicia had not lived there—as far as Izzy knew, nobody had—for years and years. Izzy had been in Portland, having her baby, when her mother had met yet another man and, this time, had followed him to God only knew where. She hadn't left a forwarding address; nor had she ever tried to get in touch with her daughter again. When Izzy had returned to Thunder Ridge, she'd contacted their old landlord, who had been one of Felicia's drinking buddies. He hadn't had a clue as to Felicia's whereabouts but had told Izzy she could do whatever she wanted with the trailer; for years he'd been meaning to sell it for scrap but hadn't gotten around to it.

"We don't have to go in this time, Latke."

Sometimes, like when she'd been getting her business degree online and had felt too tired to study for finals, she would go inside just to remind herself why she worked so hard. She was building a future for her son that would be the polar opposite of her own past. She was strong, she had values, she was not a quitter...

Today she had come simply because the pull to do so had been overwhelming. As gloomy as her memories of the years in this trailer could be, they often illuminated her present.

Crouching beside her dog, she cuddled Latke's comforting heavy folds. "You should have seen the flowers Nate put in the trees. Peonies and pink roses. It looked like a scene from *A Midsummer Night's Dream*." Latke turned her head to swipe her broad tongue across Izzy's chin.

"I love you so much, too," Izzy murmured. She rubbed Latke's ears in the way that made the dog stretch her neck forward in ecstasy. "I know why I had the panic attack at Henry and Sam's," she told her loyal companion. "It's because that night on the lake with Nate, I understood what *bashert* felt like. For the first time in my life. It was like finding out you can fly without wings."

When she was very young, she'd tried so hard to gain every ounce of affection that she could, to find someone to belong to. Before she'd had Eli, the best Thanksgiving she could remember was the one year Felicia had a boyfriend named Rick, who drove a Schwan food truck. He was a nice man, one of the few who had hung around awhile, and he'd brought over a complete Thanksgiving meal for the three of them to share, with pumpkin ice cream he'd said was especially for Izzy. The food had been completely prepared and only needed to be reheated, but Felicia had complained that staying home was "a drag" and had begun to drink. She'd managed to burn the stuffing and potatoes while Izzy and Rick had played checkers. In the end, Felicia had threatened to go out and "have some adult fun *on my own*" if Rick didn't join her. So Izzy had stayed home alone, cleaned up the mess and scooped pumpkin ice cream straight from the container while watching TV. She'd made turkey sandwiches with cranberry sauce and mayonnaise to share with her mother when she returned, but Felicia hadn't come home until two days later, and she'd scoffed at the plastic-wrapped sandwiches Izzy had pulled from the fridge. "Throw that garbage out. I broke up with Rick. What a loser."

Izzy had been entertaining fantasies that Rick was going to be her father, but no way had she been about to say that and incur Felicia's ridicule. So she'd taken the sandwiches outside, walked far away from the trailer and set the food out for any animals who might not mind Rick's offering. Then she'd sobbed until she'd thought she was going to throw up. She'd been twelve at the time.

By fifteen, she'd decided she was done with feeling so much. A coldness had seeped into her bones, and she'd welcomed it. After a while, it had seemed nothing could touch her. A perfect sunrise, a thoughtful gesture, Felicia's cruelty—it had all become the same to her. And then...

"I realized I was dying of thirst in the desert, and Nate became my rain." She gave the top of Latke's head a gentle kiss, more soothing to her than to the dog. "Yesterday, on the river, I felt that way again. With everything I have now, everyone I love, there was still a moment when I remembered what it used to be like, and..." Giving Latke a tight hug, she admitted, "I wanted Nate as badly as I wanted him before."

She looked again at the trailer. Broken, corroded.

It was hard to be courageous when you were continuously trying to fix the broken parts of you. With that thought, an odd, blanketing peace settled around her. Maybe she didn't have to do that anymore. Maybe she was already as fixed as she was going to get, and the broken bits that were left were there simply to remind her she was human.

Suddenly, she knew what she had to do.

"Come on, pancake baby. "It's time to go back to the present."

Chapter Ten

Izzy sneaked up the staff-only staircase of the Eagle's Crest Inn so that no one she knew would see her going inside Nate's room. She knew now that they would never be more than friends. She planned to tell him tonight that he had a son, and there was no way she was going to carry on an affair or a fling or even a flirtation with her teenage son's father, to whom she had been neither married nor engaged. This was not *The Gilmore Girls*. She needed to let go of the resentment, the hope, the longing, and start sort-of-over again with Nate. They needed to be teammates, players on Team Eli.

She didn't have much time, either, to make progress: Eli would be home from camp in a few days.

Screwing up her courage, she raised her fist and knocked on the door. Three rapid taps with her knuckles. Then she waited. Nothing. It was after nine in the evening. There was precious little to do at this hour in Thunder Ridge unless Nate was frequenting bars these days, or perhaps the twenty-four-hour Laundromat.

She had raised her hand to knock again just as the floor creaked. She glanced to her right.

Nate was walking down the carpeted hallway, looking right at her. He did not appear friendly.

"Hi," she said, hand lowering to her side.

He said nothing, just kept walking until he was in front of her, and she had to hop out of the way while he tucked a book under his left arm and opened his door with a card. The door remained open after he entered his bedroom suite, and Izzy had a pretty clear view of what appeared to be a studio-style apartment, with a queen-size bed, a kitchenette to the left with a small table with two chairs. A desk was placed beneath the window that overlooked the street.

Tossing his book onto the table, Nate went to the refrigerator and pulled out a bottle of water, which he opened and chugged, still with his back to her. "I assume you're here to see me," he said, replacing the bottle and shutting the refrigerator door.

Uh-oh. No more Mr. Nice Nate.

"Yes. I thought if you had time to talk, I'd like to. Talk." His demeanor was no help to her nerves, and she felt the urge to hyper-babble. Resisting the urge to speak, she waited through the difficult silence.

Opening a cabinet in the surprisingly spacious kitchen, Nate pulled out a plate, then grabbed a bag from the top of the fridge and withdrew four large cookies. Setting the dish in the center of the table, he lowered himself to a chair, nodding to the one opposite his. "Have a seat."

"All right, if you're sure."

"I'm not. But you're here."

Wow. This was a different Nate altogether than she had ever seen before. He looked the same, dressed in black denims and a sky blue polo shirt that enhanced his eyes and clung handsomely to his shoulders, chest and muscular arms. But his features looked as if they'd been carved from granite.

Izzy approached the table, pulled out the chair he'd indicated and sat. She'd dressed in a flowy, rose-colored skirt and lace-edged white tank top, thinking the ensemble made her seem approachable. The fashion equivalent of a white flag.

"You're probably wondering why I'm here."

"I'm wondering how I didn't see you in the lobby."

"Oh. There's a back staircase for the staff."

"You work here?"

"No. The Pickle Jar delivers take-out meals when someone phones from the inn. We leave our menus in the rooms, and—"

"I saw. Were you delivering a meal this evening?"

"No."

"You didn't want to be seen visiting me?"

"No," she said honestly, "I didn't want to be seen visiting you. Back when we were dating, I didn't know that many people, and they didn't know me. Now I'm kind of a fixture around town. I manage a local business, and—"

Oh, crap, she'd almost said, *I'm on the PTA*. That revelation had to wait a bit longer. "I'm pretty active in community work."

"And being seen with me would affect you…how?"

"I love Thunder Ridge."

His eyebrows rose. He remembered how desperate she'd once been to leave.

"I do love it here," she insisted. "It took leaving and coming back for me to appreciate that I can have all I want right here. I look at Thunder Ridge as my permanent home."

"No plans to leave again?"

"Nope."

He nudged the plate of chocolate chip cookies closer to her. "Help yourself."

She reached for one to give her hands something to do. "Thanks."

"I'd have gotten peanut butter if I'd known you were coming over."

He remembered that, too. "This is great. Fine. I like these."

"So, go on," he said. "You were telling me why you don't want anyone to see you with me."

"It's not that. I just don't see the point in encouraging gossip. This town has changed over the years, but in some ways it's as small as it ever was. And…" She fumbled a bit. "I'm hoping we can get to know each other again without prying eyes."

Perspiration broke out in a fine sheen on her face, which she was sure was turning bright red. After their fight at the river, he could reject her utterly. Leaning back in his chair, legs outstretched, he watched. And waited.

"I want to apologize to you for the judgments I made when we were younger. And for the judgments I made more recently, because, let's face it, it's not as if I ever stopped judging you."

His left eyebrow rose.

"Except now," she hastened to add. "I'm stopping now. You're right that we were both kids making adult decisions. It was an incredibly difficult time, and we ended badly." Izzy took a steadying breath. So far, she felt hot and prickly instead of relieved, but she was determined to finish. "I hope we can end that chapter in our lives and begin a new chapter as…as friends."

Nate was still frowning.

"Maybe," she amended, "*friends* isn't quite the right word. *Acquaintances.* We can be good acquaintances."

His eyes narrowed. "Or…people," she tried again. "Good people who…know each other."

Note to self: Should your current job end, do not consider a career in communications. Of any kind.

Nate took a bite of his cookie, considering her while he chewed. After a pregnant pause, the awkwardness of which was rivaled only by her entire three years of high school, he said, "You don't like chocolate chip cookies."

"Pardon?"

He gestured to the one untasted in her hand. "You never did like them. If we're going to be 'good acquaintances,' you need to tell me what you're really thinking."

Izzy searched for a spark of humor in his flinty eyes. "All right."

"If we move from acquaintanceship to actually being friends, I'll buy peanut butter cookies."

"Really?"

"Yes. I would do that for a friend."

"That's nice of you. Would that be the sandwich kind? With the peanut buttery filling?"

"Those are gross."

"It's what I like."

"All right, then." He licked a few crumbs from his fingers, then noted, "You never used to tell me what you wanted."

"I didn't?"

"No. You ate dozens of my famous home-baked chocolate chip cookies before you ever hinted that you preferred peanut butter."

"Well, who doesn't like famous home-baked chocolate chip cookies?"

"You. You like peanut butter with gross peanut buttery filling, so that's what you should have."

"Doesn't happiness come from being content with what

you have rather than believing you should have everything you want?"

"Of course. But the key word is *everything*. No one gets everything he wants, but you've got to believe you're worth at least some of what you want."

"Is there anything you've wanted that you haven't gotten?"

He looked at her quizzically. "Are you serious?"

"Yes. You wanted to be an architect, and you are. You wanted to live in a big, exciting city, and you do. What didn't you get?"

"I was married for five years. As hard as we tried, we couldn't make it work." He didn't have to say he considered that a failure—she could read it in his eyes.

"What happened?" Though she wasn't entirely certain she wanted to know, Izzy couldn't keep the question from popping out.

"Julianne is a great woman. An interior decorator with a successful career of her own. She's smart, beautiful, giving to her friends. And to me."

I am so sorry I asked.

"I like to think I was a good husband, too. That made it all the more confusing when we both realized we weren't happy. On paper, our marriage should have worked. Our *lives* should have worked." He shook his head. "It's true that no one has it all, but when you realize you don't feel... whole...then you know you have to make a change."

"Are you the one who wanted the divorce?"

"She asked, but I knew I shouldn't fight it. Julianne was looking for what she called 'a more authentic life.'"

"What does that mean?"

"I think it means she wanted to feel that she was where she was supposed to be. After our divorce was final, she compared her life to a three-course meal and said she was still waiting for the entrée. Obviously, she didn't think it was ever going to arrive if she stayed with me.'"

Ouch. Izzy winced on his behalf. "But how do you *know* you couldn't have made it happen, made that feeling come, if you'd stayed together? How does she even know that what she wants actually exists?"

Nate smiled. "When you walked in tonight, I had no idea we'd be having this kind of conversation. Did you?"

"No." A smile played around Izzy's lips, also. "Am I being too personal?"

"Nope." He leaned forward, forearms resting on his knees. There seemed to be an invisible beam connecting their gazes. "I can't speak for Julianne, but I think we got married in the first place hoping the feeling of emptiness would go away. This didn't go over so well the last time I told you, but I felt whole for the first time that summer before college. There was nothing I wanted, nothing I needed that I didn't already have. There was nobody I had to become."

"Don't you think that was because you'd already gotten into college? All your wheels were on the right track."

Nate shook his head. "It had nothing to do with that. I'd spent four years of high school 'on track' and never feeling like I could stop moving or striving toward something. It took me a long time to realize—longer than it should have—that I felt whole for the first time in my life that summer. Because of you."

Wow. That's almost as good as "you complete me."

Nate was going to make it hard to keep her wits about her if he said things like that.

"That was really only true over the summer, though. Don't you think?" she asked, determined to keep their relationship in perspective. "After I found out I was pregnant, I *did* hope that you would change. I wanted you to say you were ready to become a father." *And a husband.*

"You wanted to keep the baby."

Getting warmer. "Yes. I said I agreed to the adoption plan, but it wasn't what I wanted. It made sense. Of course it did. We were so young and had no way to support ourselves and a child, like you said. But I'd never had a family, not really. I didn't know what a mother's love felt like. I couldn't imagine not taking care of my baby. I wanted someone I could love completely. Someone who needed me. It was selfish of me, I know."

Nate's frown deepened. Darkening to ocean blue, his eyes seemed to hide a tempest of thoughts. "It wasn't selfish." There were more words inside, wanting to emerge, but he lowered his head, his forehead on the heels of his palms. When he looked up again, the frown was gone, but his eyes looked older, tired. "You said you'd wished I'd changed. I wish I had, too."

Whoa. He wished…that he'd been ready to be a father?

Pure longing rushed like white water through Izzy's body, over the stone around her heart, wearing it away, smoothing the rough edges.

The room pulsed with intimacy. It seemed smaller—much—than when she'd first walked in. Nate reached toward her, something she realized only when she felt him taking her hands in his and holding them. Gentle, warm, secure—his touch was all the things it used to be. Including electrifying. It was impossible not to remember in that moment that she was in his hotel room. With a bed that was bigger than anything else in the room.

They'd had sex too soon, and at first, to Izzy, it had felt like falling down a waterfall—exhilarating but frightening, with no idea at all of whether she was going to land safely or not. Once she'd given him the last bit of her heart, their lovemaking had changed to something that felt more like standing beneath the waterfall with every pore in her body dying of thirst.

And every time, he had stared at her afterward as if what they'd just shared was something rare and important. In later years, she'd wondered what it would have felt like if she'd known he loved her, too. What if every kiss, every touch, had been a promise sealing their forevers?

Nate brought his chair closer to hers. Their knees were almost touching. "I really want to kiss you." His whisper touched every cell in her body.

Dear God, help me remember why it's wrong...even though it sounds so, so right.

Eli. Eli. This is going to be hard on him...complicated... Don't make it worse.

Nate moved closer. It took every ounce of strength she possessed to squeeze the big, strong hands that held hers. She squeezed tightly. *You have no idea what's coming. You don't need more complications, either.*

"I have to go now." The soft words echoed in the silent room. "But we need to see each other again. Get to know each other better. Very soon, please."

His disappointment was palpable, the tension in his body traveling through his fingers. Raising her hands, he pressed his lips to the back of her knuckles—obviously the only kiss he figured she'd allow—and agreed, "Very soon."

Chapter Eleven

"'Double support' means both of your feet have to be touching the pavement at the same time," Derek insisted as he, Holliday and Izzy slogged back into town after an hour and a half of training for the Ridge-to-the-Coast Relay. They were participating as Team Pickle Jar, and Izzy had made T-shirts—gray with the words "Got Pickles?" underneath a smiling green dill that had arms and legs and running shoes. So far, no one but she was willing to wear the shirt.

"I didn't see both your feet on the ground at the same time once today," Derek harassed Holliday, who had been rolling her eyes more than her feet while Derek coached them.

"On the day of the race, I will be wearing my Daisy Dukes and a Got Pickles? T-shirt that I have preshrunk and cut to midriff length. No one—except you—will be looking at my feet. Guaranteed."

"You're really going to wear your Got Pickles? tee?"

Izzy exclaimed, feeling her energy return. Holliday smiled beatifically. "Thanks!" Every bit of advertising was going to help.

"You think sex is going to sell pickles?" Derek scoffed.

Both women looked at him.

"Jeepers, I'm not sure, Sheriff." Holliday mock frowned. "It's hard to tell what'll sell here in Mayberry. Hey, I know," she said, and her expression cleared. "Let's ask Opie!"

Derek's scowl intensified. He hated Holliday's periodic references to the old *Andy Griffith Show.* She'd accused him more than once of trying to keep Thunder Ridge in the dark ages with his old-fashioned values. The town-hall lecture he had given the previous month on the perils of littering, jaywalking and other misdemeanors—complete with a pie chart he'd labeled Small Crimes, Big Fines— hadn't helped matters.

"The Pickle Jar is a family restaurant," he said. "That's what I'm saying. Izzy doesn't want to confuse the customers. Do you, Izz?"

"Oh. Uh, well...no," she agreed at Derek's thunderous expression, "of course not. Although, you know, it might not *confuse* them exactly. And Holly is the local librarian. There's an implied wholesomeness right there."

"Wholesome?" both Holliday and Derek protested, but then Holly turned to the sheriff and growled, "Watch it, pal. I'm a county employee, too."

Izzy shook her head and moved on as the bickering continued. Who cared if Holly wore cutoffs and showed her midriff? It was hard to confuse customers who didn't exist.

As they walked past Burger-ology, one of Thunder Ridge's newer venues, Izzy's mood dropped a bit. Okay, a ton. Burger-ology, which was decorated in fire-engine red, cloud white and sleek chrome, appeared to be doing a bang-up lunch business. When she'd phoned The Pickle Jar at the end of their walk, Willa had answered and admitted that lunch had been slow.

"I'm thirsty after all that walking," she said, changing the channel in her mind. There would be time to obsess about work after she showered and returned to the deli. "Anybody feel like getting an ice-cream soda?"

Thankfully, both of her friends agreed, and they all headed to The General Store. A couple of blocks away from the small market and soda fountain, they could see a large crowd gathered outside. The sound of raised voices made Derek pick up the pace while Izzy and Holliday jogged behind.

"Raybald, you nutcase! Come down from there, you hear me?" Jax Stewart, owner of The General Store, stood at the front of the crowd, shading his eyes as he looked up. "This is my building. And I do not want you hanging off the second story."

"I rent this second story, and I know my rights. This barber pole is *my* property. I can be out here if I want to be! I can sing 'America the Beautiful' if I want to. In fact, I think I will. 'Oh, beautiful for spacious skies—'"

Ron Raybald had, from what Izzy could see, tied himself to the striped pole outside the window of his second-floor barbershop.

"What the devil—" Pushing through the crowd, Derek shouted above the chatter, "Ron! What the heck are you doing?" Ron continued to sing. Derek turned to Jax. "What's he doing?"

"Sealing his fate. He's going to wind up in a loony bin for the rest of his sorry life!" The latter part of Jax's statement was yelled at Ron, who responded by singing louder.

Pinching the bridge of his nose, Derek lowered his head. "Can anybody here tell me what is going on? Where's Russell?"

Russell was one of Derrick's deputies.

"He went up the Ridge," Jonas Bates, owner of the hardware store, called out in the creaky voice that reminded Izzy of the rusty nails Jonas always advocated replacing. "Two summer skiers got into a tussle on the chairlift, so Russ went to sort them out. But I can tell you what's going on." He pointed to Jax. "Jax gave Ron a notice saying he's planning to remodel the building, and Ron thinks that's going to hurt business."

In the middle of a rousing "and crown thy good," Ron abruptly stopped singing and said, "I was not worried about business! I'm not thinking about myself. It's my civic duty to protest the destruction of culturally relevant structures. I am a member of the Thunder Ridge Historical Society."

"Hysterical Society is more like it," Jax sniped. "And I am not destroying the building, you rabble-rouser, I'm improving it."

"Words, words, words," Ron sang. "That's all I hear is meaningless words."

"Come on down, I'll give you something meaningful," Jax shouted.

"That's enough, both of you!" While Derek attempted to calm the storm, Izzy motioned to Holliday that she was heading home. When Eli wasn't around, she rarely stayed away from the restaurant.

"What's going on?"

Izzy looked up. Nate greeted her, his expression open and relaxed, a contrast from when she last saw him. In perfectly cut jeans and a crisp white T-shirt that highlighted the classic V of his torso, he emitted the same golden-boy aura she'd sensed the first time she'd ever laid eyes on him.

He'd certainly changed, though. If people were cars, Nate would have been a Mustang in high school—sporty, fast, cool. As an adult, he was a Jaguar—powerful yet smooth, confident but not pretentious, great looking with substance.

"Sidewalk sale?" he inquired humorously as they met at the curb.

"No, just a difference of opinion between Jax Stewart and Ron Raybald."

"Jax?" One of Nate's ridiculously well-shaped black brows arched. "That's who I'm coming to see. What's happening between him and Ron?"

Briefly, Izzy described the conflict. "Jax and Ron are reflecting what's going on all over town. Half the people are screaming for progress—a new cell tower, more modern shops, a fast-food restaurant—and the other half want everything to stay the way it is, because they're afraid to lose the sweetness of the town."

Nate nodded slowly, thoughtfully. "It *is* a sweet place. More run-down than I remembered it, though. Is it realistic to keep it the way it is?"

"It's always been run-down. You're probably noticing it more because you've been away."

"Which side of the divide do you stand on? Are you a fan of progress or preservation?"

"Both, I suppose. I see the value of remodeling the older buildings, but people like Ron can't afford to close down during construction. And Jax can. He's inherited quite a few properties around town. Ron thinks Jax would be happy to close him down so he can have the whole building, because when Jax's grandfather owned the building, he gave Ron a ninety-nine-year lease. Now that Jax has inherited the business and the property, some people think Jax would like to force Ron and a few other tenants out."

"That doesn't sound like Jax. He's a good man."

A kernel of memory popped in Izzy's brain. Nate and Jax had played football together. Like Nate, Jax had moved away after high school, but he'd returned a few years ago with a business degree.

"In addition to inheriting, Jax has been buying properties all over Thunder Ridge, from what I understand. A lot of business people are renting from him now. It's understandable that they're fidgety, wondering what he has in mind. He's not endearing himself to people by dissing the local Historical Society."

Nate pulled out his phone and started texting, then slipped it into his back pocket and smiled at Izzy. "Want to get something to drink?"

"I thought you were here to see Jax."

"I just told him we can reschedule. Sounds like he's busy." Nate's gaze skimmed Izzy. "You still look good in shorts."

Instantly, she felt self-conscious. Her hand rose to her hair, which was damp with perspiration. "I'm a sweaty mess."

Nate shook his head. "Women never understand what turns a man on."

"Sweat?"

He took a step closer as Jax and Ron's audience started to disperse. "Passion. Drive. You look like you were very driven today. Plus, you're wearing a Got Pickles? T-shirt."

"And that's hot?"

"Oh, yeah."

Awareness sizzled inside Izzy. The anticipation of what they would say next tasted like champagne. She jumped as a hand patted her back.

"Hi, there," Holliday said. She draped herself over Izzy's shoulder. "Derek went up to the barbershop to unhook Ron from the pole. Ron can't get the knots out of the rope he used. Jax is getting a pair of gardening shears. There's just never a dull moment around here." She sent a dazzling smile from Nate to Izzy and back again.

"Nate Thayer, I heard you were back!" An older gentleman Izzy did not recognize pumped Nate's hand while clapping him on the upper arm.

While the two men started chatting, Holliday whispered to Izzy, "He's been ogling your legs."

"No, he hasn't. Really?"

"Yes, indeed. Are you two getting together right now?"

"No, I was going to go home."

"Alone?"

Her tone was so insinuating Izzy felt a chuckle in her chest. "Yes, you scary sex addict, alone. I have something serious to discuss with him, remember?"

"You're allowed to talk during sex."

"Didn't you recommend remaining calm, cool and collected during my encounters with Nate? 'Keep a cool head. Keep your emotions under control'—that's what you said."

"I'm always calm, cool and collected during sex. Besides, I told you all that before I saw the way Tall, Dark and *Deee*licious looks at you. Now I think you should have sex *and* tell him he's the father of your child."

"Shh," Izzy pleaded, even though Holly's voice was already a murmur. "I'm not that girl anymore. No sex until—"

"The afterlife?"

"Hilarious. No. No sex until Eli is out of the house, and I find someone to share the rest of my life with."

"With the magic Mr. Right? What if you never find him? Birds do it, bees do it, even girls in pickle tees can do it."

"Very funny."

"And it rhymes."

"Shh, here he is again."

Nate's conversation wrapped up, and he returned to the women, but as he opened his mouth to speak, an elderly female voice exclaimed, "Izzy, darling, my lawn looks like an Old English sheepdog. Is Eli available to mow?"

Holliday's arm tightened around Izzy's shoulders even as Izzy tightened up all over.

"Hi, Evelyn!" she said to the eightysomething redhead, who approached with single-minded determination. *I can't think of anything else to say*, Izzy thought in blind panic. She looked at Holliday, who also appeared stumped.

Wearing a lightweight pale pink jogging suit, Evelyn stopped directly in front of them. "Darling, I know it's summer, but I'm still watering my lawn, and it's growing like wildfire. When can Eli come over?"

Oh, dear lord. This was not how she wanted Nate to find out he had a son. "Right. Well, Evelyn, I think, um… Didn't he tell you? He went out of town. I think he'll be available again next week. I'll have to check my calendar. My yard's a mess, too!" Good! She'd made him sound like a gardener. Holliday gave her an approving squeeze.

Evelyn, however, gave her a strange look. "You think he'll be available? Don't you know? I don't approve of all this not-knowing what goes on these days. Honey, Eli is still only—"

"He is still the only person I'd trust with my lawn," Holliday interrupted, releasing Izzy and flinging her arm around Evelyn instead, "if I had one." She began leading the woman away. "Evelyn, did I tell you the books you put on hold are in? There are three other holds, though, on *Hip Hop for Dummies*, so we should pick that up for you right away."

"Ooh. All right, I don't want to lose that one. But you'll call me?" she asked Izzy anxiously over her shoulder.

"Yes. Very soon."

Faintly bemused, Nate commented. "Sounds like Thunder Ridge could use a few good landscapers."

"Yeah." Emitting a high, ridiculous-sounding laugh,

Izzy grabbed Nate's elbow and propelled him across the street. *I have got to tell him before he finds out from somebody else.* As they stepped up on the opposite curb, in front of the park, she announced, "I don't have to work tonight. I was thinking about driving into Portland to…" *It was summer—what was going on in Portland?* "To… go to…the…summer concert series! At the zoo. Remember those?"

"Yeah, of course. I saw Earth, Wind and Fire there."

"Wow. Well, tonight is—" *Oh, crumbs.* She had no idea who was playing at the zoo tonight. *Don't get specific. Keep it general.* "Who knows who's playing? So, would you like to? Go with me? To the concert?"

If a bobblehead doll could speak, it would sound exactly like me. She wasn't entirely surprised when Nate studied her dubiously a moment, then said, "I'll walk you home."

So, that would be a no?

Great. Now she was going to have to figure out another time to tell him, and she preferred to be away from Thunder Ridge when she did it.

Taking the lead, she walked beside him, silent as the sun warming their skin. Nate looked enviably cool, but Izzy could smell his skin. Perhaps it was more memory than reality, but he had that yummy Nate's-skin scent that used to make her want to snuggle into him and stay there indefinitely.

Nate seemed as content to walk without speaking, beyond the streets that formed the center of town, and into the residential area where she shared the little cottage with—

Oh, fudgeknuckles. She couldn't invite Nate in—there were photos of Eli everywhere. Three houses away from her own place, Izzy slowed down, trying to remember if any of her son's things—bike helmet, basketball, mud-caked size-nine hiking boots—were on the front porch.

Well, it would be a conversation starter, she reasoned,

but, oh, my goodness, her head and heart were pounding in unison.

At the border of her yard, which Eli had mowed and edged before he'd left for camp, she saw that the porch was clear of everything except two deck chairs, a single low table and an umbrella stand.

"This is me." She gestured to the house, abruptly aware of how proud she was of her little place.

Her cottage might be tiny by most standards, but it was a cheerful butter yellow. The creamy white trim had been repainted just last summer, and oversize wood-and-chrome wind chimes flanked a huge hanging basket of bright pink fuchsias. *Happy people live here.* That was what the front of her house said.

Briefly, Izzy closed her eyes. *Please let happy people continue to live here.*

Nate studied the building, his gaze roving up, down, left and right. She wondered if he was looking at it as an architect. If so, he could no doubt catalog a host of changes he would make. Izzy's stomach dropped as once again she realized Nate would be able to give Eli so many more of the things that mattered to a teenage boy, including, she was sure, swanky digs and his own state-of-the-art gadget-filled bedroom.

She was just about to picture the moment that Eli was going to tell her he wanted to move to Chicago when Nate commented, "Great place. It suits you."

"I bought it myself," she said, allowing pride to infuse her voice. "Well, not entirely. Henry and Sam helped with the down payment, but I finished paying them back last year."

Surprise and respect infused his expression. "That's quite an accomplishment."

Pleasure began to fill her until she remembered that it had taken the entire past decade to repay the ten thousand dollars. She shook her head, appreciative but realistic.

"You're being nice. You know darn well the down payment for this house is probably what you spend on a summer vacation. Come on, let's sit on the porch."

He grabbed her hand, pulling her back until he was looking directly in her eyes. "Buying your own home—any home—is a tremendous achievement. And your house is lovely." Her hand was still clasped in his, the pressure of his fingers firm and steady and warm. "You should be proud as hell of what you've accomplished."

Without waiting for a response, he headed for the porch, releasing her only as they took their seats. Escaping the direct sunshine was a relief as it was still blisteringly hot with no breeze, and Izzy knew she ought to offer Nate a drink.

I wonder if he'd mind sipping from the garden hose.

"Have you made good memories here?"

She cleared her throat. "I have, yes. Very good." She drew a shallow breath. Should she tell him now?

A butterfly flitted around the flowers she'd planted in front of the porch railing. Izzy was strongly tempted to pretend it was a normal afternoon. If they'd never broken up…

I'd take his hand again.

And tell him how nervous I feel about Eli going to college in a few years with a hearing loss.

He'd tell me not to worry, that our son can handle it and we'll both be there to help him when he needs it. He'd say we can get through anything as long as we're together.

And I would believe him.

Izzy chewed her bottom lip. Dandy. Just dandy. Apparently, it didn't matter how smart she got or how strictly the school of life educated her, she was always going to be that girl who wanted a hero to come along—even though she was a single mother, and it was far, far too late for fairy tales.

"I'd like to go to the concert with you tonight."

There was a "but" in Nate's voice that made Izzy's head swivel in his direction.

"First, you should know why I want to go."

Sounded ominous. "Because you like outdoor concerts?" she tried, hoping to keep the mood light for a while longer, at least.

Humor tugged at his lips. Briefly. Then he looked serious again. "I like you. I'd like to get to know you again."

She tried to swallow. A heart couldn't literally jump into a person's throat, could it?

"How about if we start fresh, pretend we just met?" he asked. His voice dropped to a hum as soothing as the rustle of the breeze through the maple leaves. "Do you think we could do that tonight?"

Mesmerized, feeling reality begin to fade away, she nodded.

No, don't nod. You can't pretend that.

But he had her at "I like you."

Her conscience protested. *Tell him. He needs to know. Get it over with. Tell him now.*

"Nate," she began, "maybe it would be best if…"

He wagged his head, touching two fingers lightly to her lips. "Think less." It was a request. A favor. "This one time."

No. Way.

"Okay," she breathed. "Okay, let's just go to the concert."

Augggghhh!

He reached out, grasping the arms of the wicker chair in which she was seated. With little effort, he scooted it toward him, turning his own chair at the same time until they were close enough for Nate to reach behind her with his free hand and cup the back of her head. She could see tiny flecks of brown in the sea of his blue irises and the infinitesimal scar high on his right cheek from the case of chicken pox he'd had when he was five.

"On second thought, you really should know my intentions before we set the plans for tonight in stone." His voice was so soft.

Her heart beat so hard she could barely draw the breath to speak. "What are your intentions?"

She saw him moving ever closer to her lips but didn't think he was actually going to kiss her, or she'd have moved. Of course.

Or...not.

Oh. My. Goodness. How could she have forgotten this, as if her bones were melting like butter? The touch of his lips, the scent of his skin...

It was a homecoming.

Tenderly, his lips settled on hers, soft as down. She raised her hands to touch his neck, first just with her fingertips, but as the kiss deepened, her hands delved into his hair, and she was kissing him back with yearning and passion and a hunger she couldn't satisfy on a neighborhood porch.

It will never be enough. Oh, this was an exquisite, magnificent mistake.

Nate had his hands around her waist and was pulling her toward him so that she sat on the edge of her chair, their knees tangling. His kiss grew more insistent before he drew away, lowering his chin until their foreheads touched.

He swallowed. "So, do you want to?"

Izzy licked her lips. Her eyes remained closed. "Do I want to...?"

"Set our date in stone?"

Date. They shouldn't call it a date—

Shut up.

"Stone is good."

Chapter Twelve

If Izzy worried about awkward silences on the hour-long ride to Portland, she needn't have. Nate kept the mood light with anecdotes about his recent attempts to join a recreational football league.

"Some of the guys were straight out of college or still in, but they had injuries and couldn't play competitively anymore."

With one hand on the steering wheel and his right resting on the stick shift, he was the picture of relaxation. He'd insisted on driving and had picked her up in a rental car that cost several times the price of her very well-used four-wheel-drive wagon, which was practical as all getout but did nothing to enhance her sex appeal. Nate, on the other hand, looked like an ad for *Motor Trend* Sports Car of the Year.

"So, I figured I could play ball with these guys, flash some moves, but the very first scrimmage, I fall and realize I've messed up my wrist. I am the oldest guy there,

and no way am I going to admit that I sprained my wrist
and don't want to play anymore."

"What did you do?"

"Acted like a macho jerk until the pain was so bad, I
started to cry."

"You cried?"

"In front of several very large football players who probably dislocated their shoulders on a regular basis and never
noticed it. They thought I was a wuss."

His grin practically tugged her to him. Izzy wanted to
smooth her fingers over his forehead. Instead, she kept her
hands on her denim capris. "You're not a wuss."

Nate laughed. "You're too kind."

"What happened next?"

"I limped to my car, got an X-ray and a very tall beer
and went back to the gym from then on instead of to the
football field."

"You quit your team?"

"Oh, yeah."

"Did they try to talk you out of it?"

"Oh, no."

A fizzy warmth tickled her chest. Seeing the vulnerable, imperfect side of Nate was a new experience. In high
school, his success at sports, at academics and in the social realm had seemed effortless.

Izzy hadn't told anyone that Nate had kissed her today.
Hadn't stopped thinking about it, either.

When she lapsed into a fantasy that included her, Nate
and Eli together, she would forcefully wipe it from her
mind. She was getting so good, she could complete the
"wonder, drop it, wonder some more" cycle in about three
minutes, then start up again with barely a break.

Instead of taking Highway 26 to their destination, Nate
asked Izzy if she would mind his taking Burnside through
downtown and up to Washington Park, where the Oregon

Zoo sat like a hilltop village. Along the way, he asked her about all the places that had been remodeled or built during his absence, and she understood that he was viewing downtown Portland with the eye of a commercial architect. At eighteen, when they'd ventured into the city, he had dreamed aloud of someday constructing skyscrapers.

"You made it come true," she said, letting the awe truly sink in. She'd spent so much time resenting him she hadn't really considered his achievements. "You build skyscrapers."

"Yes, I do."

His tone was hard to read, so she probed, "You must feel crazy proud when you drive by one of your buildings."

His fingers curled around the wheel. "I thought I would." A muscle worked in his jaw before he spoke again. "In school, I wanted to focus on sustainable design for large commercial projects. But when my parents moved to Chicago after my father's heart attack, it hit home that they were getting older and needed more help, so I started taking jobs. Anything I could get in a field related to architecture. One of the companies I worked for hired me right out of school, and I never looked back." He shook his head. "I never looked around, either."

"That seems reasonable. Under the circumstances."

"Yeah." He shrugged. "Dreams and circumstance make interesting dance partners. I haven't found the rhythm."

Izzy stared at him, stunned. "Are you saying you're not happy with your career?"

They were just passing Powell's City of Books, and he glanced at the multilevel store as he answered. "I have no right not to be happy. I've had plenty of opportunities that others haven't." He gave her a sidelong look from behind his Ray-Bans. "I do realize that. But if I'm being a hundred percent honest, I feel disappointed a lot of the time." His lips twisted. "Don't say it."

"What?"

"'You're a spoiled brat, Thayer.'"

Was she thinking that? She certainly *had* thought it, once upon a time. "I've never called you 'Thayer.'"

He laughed, appreciating the irony. Then he remembered. "Yeah, you did call me 'Thayer' once. Remember the day we had a picnic at Trillium Lake, and you bet me the last five potato chips that you could spell more nine-letter words beginning with *S* than I could?"

She frowned. "Vaguely."

"And, because I knew how much you loved barbecue potato chips, I magnanimously allowed you to win, after which you said, 'Hand me the bag, Thayer.'"

"You remember that?"

"I remember because you didn't even want to share."

"Well, you eat more potato chips than I do. And you did not magnanimously let me win."

"Did, too."

"You did not."

"I thought you said you only vaguely remember this."

"It's coming back to me. I won with *salacious*. I earned those chips."

He shrugged. "Guess we'll never know. Unless you want a rematch. You still love barbecue chips?"

"As long as they're ripple."

"Thought so. I brought a bag."

Just as with the cookies, she was absurdly touched that he remembered little details about her.

"And gummy worms mixed with popcorn." Grimacing, he shook his head. "Do you still eat that?"

"Only when I go to the movies. Or watch one at home. Or think about watching a movie either in the theater or at home."

"Even though I worry about the sanity of anyone who would eat that—"

Our son loves it.

"—I brought you some nonetheless. So, rematch while we wait for the concert to start?"

"Okay."

As they left the city proper and headed into the wooded majesty of Washington Park, she recalled the other times they'd made this drive, in his battered pickup. The last time had been the evening she'd told him she was pregnant. "Why does your life disappoint you?" she asked. "What are you disappointed in, exactly?"

Navigating the turns in the road up to the zoo, Nate seemed to think carefully about his reply. "Some of it is obvious, I suppose. I want to design commercial buildings that are environmentally sound. And I want their exterior design to be harmonious with the surroundings rather than overpowering. But I have a secure job, and I have financial responsibilities, even though I'm not always on the same page as the people who commission building plans." He flicked his gaze at her. "That sounds like a cop-out, even to me."

She offered a small smile. "Not necessarily. I know about making choices based on responsibilities. Is there anything besides career that disappoints you?"

He hesitated only a moment. "When you get up each morning, do you have a sense of purpose, Izzy?"

Whoa. "Yes." *I have your son.* "I feel responsible to Henry and Sam, all the employees at The Pickle Jar. I suppose the fact that the restaurant is always struggling gives me a sense of purpose." She wrinkled her nose. "I never thought about that before. It's kind of a paradox, isn't it? Maybe if we were a great success, I wouldn't feel so driven. Do you think that's your problem? You're too successful?"

Nate didn't smile. "Maybe."

He turned the car into the entrance of Washington Park, where dense foliage in a dozen shades of green gave it a magical, almost otherworldly feel, protected and safe from the slings and arrows of the city below. That was how she had felt with Nate. "I loved that summer with you," she said quietly. "It didn't seem to have anything to do with the rest of my life. I guess that's what you've been saying, too. So maybe that's what we were?" She shrugged, still trying to figure it out after all these years. "Each other's escape?"

He frowned mightily. "Maybe." The word sounded heavy, reluctant.

"The problem was that real life intruded, and the bubble burst."

On their right was a small parking lot in front of a clearing used for archery practice. Nate pulled the car into a space, unclicked his seat belt and turned to her. "You think it's that straightforward?"

She nodded. "Yes. We were kids. What did we know?" She tried to laugh. "What do kids ever know about romance? We barely know ourselves at that age."

"Maybe we knew more then than we do now," he suggested, leaning forward.

Just like this afternoon, his eyes and the expression in them mesmerized her, but she was determined to keep her wits about her. She shook her head. "It's a fact that the human mind isn't fully formed until a person reaches his twenties, you know. There's a lot of research on this. Until then, people don't have the, um…"

Was he moving closer?

"…the capacity to, uh…the capability to think clearly and be logical and…"

He *was* moving closer.

"…not impulsive, so they shouldn't be having relationships."

"I don't think it's that simple."

"Yes." She nodded emphatically. "Yes, it is. What's simple is abstention. We should abstain from relationships. Focus on school."

"Tall order." His voice dropped to that low hum that made her stomach buzz. "What if you meet the right person early in your life?"

"Well, then you…wait. You wait."

Nate reached for her, his warm, warm hand on the back of her neck, making every hair on her nape tingle and stand on end. For years, she'd been using her mind to override her emotions. She knew how to take control of her body and, except when it came to Eli, of her heart, as well. But now Nate kissed her, and it left her brain spinning.

She kissed him back. Her palms rested on his chest. When she found the strong thud of his heartbeat, her body trembled, years of yearning pushing against the dam she'd built to hold back her desire. It was easy not to respond to other men. Not so with Nate.

Just a little more, her body begged. *We'll stop in a second. Honest.*

It took several seconds, however, and Nate was the one who pulled back. Not, she noticed, without effort.

"It is not," he repeated his earlier words, "that simple."

This time, she agreed.

If viewed aerially, the concert lawn at the Oregon Zoo would doubtlessly resemble an undulating sea of people, all milling about as they searched for seats, got in line for shave ice or ordered bento boxes, or bratwurst and beer from one of the tents set up around the venue. Nate held Izzy's hand as they wove through the bodies preparing to listen to Chicago perform their greatest hits. The atmosphere was as festive as a Fourth of July, but no matter how many other people were present, Izzy's attention remained solely on Nate. Or, more specifically, on his hand. Because just holding hands with him was more exciting than anything she'd experienced in years, and she was kind of curious about the delicious sensation, since a hand was a hand was a hand.

Except that Nate's hand—the feel of his palm and his fingers—made her feel 100 percent safe and warm and loved. And for once, she wasn't even worried about that.

I should be completely freaked out.

But she understood that this perfect sensation was temporary. Maybe that was what made the feeling okay. This time, she wasn't going to be surprised when it ended.

Just a little bit longer, and then I'll find the right moment to tell him about Eli, and after that...

Disappointment, sharp and sudden, tugged her heart down like an anchor. Once she told Nate about Eli, they would have to stop thinking about themselves, pull up their big-parent panties and pour all their energies into learning how to co-parent a teenage son.

Co-parent. Such a grown-up, modern word.

Tiny needles of dread pricked her skin from the inside out.

"You okay?" Nate turned his head in question as they cut through a line of people at one of the beer tents.

Sick to her stomach, she nodded. *What if he wants Eli to move to Chicago? What if Eli wants to go? What if his mother still doesn't accept Eli, or if she can't accept his hearing loss? What if Eli feels terrible about himself after meeting his father? What if he feels terrible about me? What if—*

"You're cutting my circulation off, Izzy." When they reached a bit of a clearing, he faced her, holding up their hands. "My fingers are blue. What's up?"

"Fear of crowds."

"Really? Is that something new?"

"I guess." He surveyed the scene around them. "Did you see the sold-out sign when we came in? There are probably more people here than usual. Do you want to leave? Walk around the park instead?"

"No." The music would start soon, and it would be too difficult to talk, and that would buy her time to calm down.

Coward, her conscience chided.

Bite me.

"Would you like to get something to eat?" They'd been forced to leave their snacks in the car when they'd realized no outside food or drinks were allowed during the concert. "Or some wine before we sit down?"

Izzy's stomach recoiled at the thought of food, and while a small wine buzz sounded tempting, she knew better than to dull her wits when she needed them more than ever. Frantic for something to do, however, she blurted, "Shave ice. I'd love a shave ice."

Nate led her to the long line in front of the tent where multihued ridges of ice were served with fat straws to sip sweet, frosty liquid that came in myriad flavor combinations. She and Nate stood side by side, their hands still clasped. There was no chance they were going to lose each other standing in line, and Izzy grew self-conscious. Should she let go first? Their hands were just hanging there, together, as if they were dating.

"Bet I know what you're going to order." He grinned.

Izzy glanced at the board with flavors scrawled over it. "How do you know what I'm going to order? I don't even know." Coconut, mango, chocolate, leche, Thai tea, banana, Northwest Marionberry—the list of flavor options went on and on.

"I know you won't be able to make up your mind. So you'll order what they're having." He nodded to a group of teenagers leaving the tent with their mountainous treats painted a rainbow of flavors. The colors bled together, one skinny stripe huddled so closely next to its neighbor that not a single flavor would be discernible.

Ha! He didn't know her as well as he thought. Years ago, she might have hungrily tried everything, like the teens, but these days, she knew that insisting on having all she wanted could end in a terrible gut ache.

"Actually, I think I'd rather have just one or two flavors." She pointed as a cup mounded with a creamy-looking, two-colored treat topped with toasted coconut passed by. "Like that one—" *Oh*.

Oh, no.

No, no, no. It couldn't be.

Squinting after the T-shirted young man who was walking away from her, Izzy sent up a quick prayer that her eyes were, in fact, deceiving her. That kid looked just like Gabe Pentzel, one of Eli's classmates, which wouldn't be so horrible, except that Gabe was a junior counselor this summer at the same inner-city camp as Eli.

Izzy's eyes darted throughout the tent. Up ahead in line, she spotted a group of younger kids dressed similarly to the boy she'd thought was Gabe, in shorts and red tees with white lettering. She squinted but couldn't make out the words on their shirts.

"Thanks for inviting me tonight," Nate said, squeezing her hand briefly. "This was a good idea. The venue's a lot more elaborate than I remember."

"Yeah, it is." Distracted, she watched another couple of red T-shirters leave the tent with their shave ices. They were younger than Eli; Izzy didn't recognize them. She strained to read their shirts. *Camp*...

She couldn't see clearly, but unless the circle of white lettering said Crimp Innards Critter, it was a darn good bet she was looking at the Camp Inner City kids. And that meant...

Her heart skittered like a pack of marbles rolling down stairs.

"You know," she turned to Nate, "I think this was *not* such a good idea, after all. It's so crowded."

Concern filled Nate's expression.

"Why don't we walk around the park like you suggested?" She would take him to the International Rose Test Garden. That was where she'd told him about Eli the first time. There was a kind of poetic full circle-ness to the idea of going back to the same bench to tell him again that he was a father. She should have thought of that before.

"Let's go." This time, she pulled Nate as she wove them through the crowds. Each time she saw a cluster of red shirts, she switched direction. "Excuse me…pardon us…" The flow of traffic was against them, the crowds growing ever thicker as showtime neared.

Her forehead perspired as they reached the edge of the concert lawn. The Africafe, a large concrete hut that served sandwiches and fries, was ahead of them, and there were fewer people congregated there. They could follow the concrete walkway that circled the building and then head to the parking lot.

Izzy wondered if Nate felt the slickness of her palm. Yuck. Her mind lurched ahead to what would happen when they got to the Rose Garden. She had pictures of Eli on her phone, of course. She would show them to Nate. Text him a few, if he wanted. Would he want that? And she would have to explain about the hearing impairment and decide how to tell Eli his father was here in town and that she'd never actually told him she was keeping their child…

There was a tug on her hand. Nate had stopped moving. She turned to see him looking at her in deep concern. Letting go of her sweaty hand, he stepped forward until he was standing over her, a half foot taller than she, holding her shoulders.

"Breathe, sweetheart. You're okay, crowd or no crowd." He inhaled deeply, urging her to do the same. "Just breathe."

Filled with compassion, his eyes reminded her of Henry's words: *Finding your* bashert *doesn't necessarily make life easier, it makes it better.*

Except that regarding her and Nate, the situation between them was the cause of her current distress, and she was about to complicate his life exponentially.

"Nate. I have something I want to say. There's something you should—"

"Hey, Mrs. L!"

Beside her, a young boy almost as tall as Nate appeared. His smile revealed braces that could not detract from his good looks. He wore the red Camp Inner City T-shirt and baggy basketball shorts with Thunder Ridge High colors.

Trey.

Their son's best friend was standing before them.

Chapter Thirteen

Suddenly, Izzy's tongue felt too large for her mouth. She'd known Trey Richards since he'd been a scrawny seven-year-old with a perpetual grin and infectious laugh.

"Are you here for the concert?" Trey asked. "Did Eli know you were coming? He didn't say anything. He's inside, getting a burger with the some of the team—that's what we call the kids in our group. The rest of the team's over there." He gestured with his chin to a group of young people sitting in the bleachers, reaching into bags of fries. "They're with the captain—that's what we call the senior counselors." Genuine and unaffected, Trey had always talked a blue streak. After the cochlear implant that allowed him to hear, Eli had joked that it had been easier to be friends with Trey when he was deaf, but the boys had been inseparable since second grade. "Yeah, so you want me to go inside and tell Eli you're out here? We're not supposed to call parents unless there's an emergency, but this is probably an exception, right?"

The prospect of her son meeting Nate like this, with no warning at all, helped Izzy find her voice. "No, Trey, don't bother. I had no idea you'd all be here tonight." Abruptly, she realized Nate's hands had dropped away from her shoulders. "We're just leaving, in fact."

"Oh."

Izzy saw him give Nate a good look for the first time. Eli's friends never saw her with a man other than Derek, or Henry and Sam.

"Hi." Shifting his bag of food, Trey stuck his right hand out to Nate. "I'm Trey."

Izzy held her breath as the two hands clasped, and her "date" responded, "Nate. Good to meet you."

"Sorry," she murmured, for failing to introduce them. Was it her imagination or did Nate's voice sound tight? "Enjoy the concert," she told Trey, beginning to walk away from the venue. "See you soon."

"Okay. Thanks."

Trey was still standing there watching her and Nate quizzically when she turned away and headed for the exit as fast as her legs and the crowd would allow. As Nate fell into step beside her, she dared a glance from beneath her lashes. His jaw looked like granite. Gazing straight ahead, he appeared to be deep in thought. They made it all the way to the car without speaking.

He opened her door, she slid in, and he walked around to the driver's side, still stone-faced and silent as she tried to figure out how to open the conversation once they reached the International Rose Test Garden. But he didn't start the car.

"You have a child," he said, part statement and part question.

"Yes."

"A son?"

She nodded, looking at him, though he was staring out the windshield. "Eli."

Nate's Adam's apple dipped. "And he's a teenager. Like Trey."

Thud...thud...thud. Her heart knocked against her chest. Apparently, they were going to have this conversation here. And even though she'd had days to think about what she was going to say, she had no idea how to make this news less...shocking.

"Eli is—" she swallowed hard "—fourteen."

There was stone-cold quiet until Nate slammed his palm on the steering wheel so hard the car shook. "Damn it! Don't make me ask all the questions. Just tell me."

With the windows rolled up and the temperature reaching eighty in the shade, the car was stifling. A deep breath was impossible, but Izzy managed a shallow one and plunged ahead.

"I didn't have a miscarriage. The last time I saw your parents, I told them I didn't want to give up my baby. I thought we...you and I...might be able to make it work. They were scared. I can see that now, especially with Eli not so far away from the age I was when I got pregnant." She wiped the perspiration from her face. "Can we roll down a window?"

He obliged. "Go on."

"Your parents reminded me of all the reasons I shouldn't be thinking about keeping the baby, and, of course, they were right. But I wasn't going to change my mind."

"You didn't tell me."

He pushed the words through gritted teeth, reminding her of a volcano preparing to erupt.

"No. I saw a photo of you at a party. It looked like a wedding or something formal, and you were grinning at the camera with your arm around a beautiful blonde girl. The previous few weeks, you hadn't had time to talk to me. It looked like...it *felt* like...you'd moved on with your life. I didn't belong in your new world, and you didn't belong back in Thunder Ridge." She tried not to allow the past hurt to infiltrate her tone, but she wasn't sure she was successful. That memory had always been painful.

Nate shook his head, his expression equal parts bafflement and ferocity. "I don't know what photo you're talking about. Or what party, but the situation wasn't about just you and me and who belonged in what world. It stopped being about you and me the instant you decided to raise a baby that was mine."

"Right. It became about *the baby*. I wasn't going to involve a birth father who didn't want him and grandparents who thought he was ruining their son's future."

"You never gave me a choice!"

There was no doubt about it; she had become the enemy. Pain welled up. She tried to stay calm. "You had a choice. For months you had a choice. I may not have done everything perfectly, but don't rewrite history, Nate. You didn't want a baby."

"And at the time, you said you agreed we weren't ready."

"We weren't! No one's ready for a baby at that age. But we were having one anyway." Pressing her fingers to her temples, she shook her head. "I told you, I never wanted to make an adoption plan. I went along with it hoping everyone would change their minds."

"When it looked like that wasn't going to happen, was that when you said you'd had a miscarriage?"

Heavy censure stained his voice. Once, she might have reveled in correcting him, happily placing the blame for the lie about the miscarriage squarely at the feet of his mother.

Now, though, she, too, was the mother of a teenager with a future more promising than her own, and she understood the desire to protect her son. *I hope I'd go about it differently.*

"Communication between your mother and me wasn't the best," she said carefully. "I think she misunderstood what I was telling her."

"Which was?"

"That I was going to keep the baby and raise him myself." She met his eyes to deliver the final truth. "And that I didn't want anything more to do with you or your family."

Nate's fingers curled tightly around the steering wheel. "And you came to that decision because I didn't have time to talk as you would have liked?" Resentment dripped from his tone. Put that way, she seemed immature and petty.

"It was partly that, yes." Only scrupulous honesty would suffice at this point. "When I saw the photo, I was sure you didn't want to be with me, with us."

"Where did you see this mystery photo?"

"Your mother showed it to me."

"A picture of me at a party." He lifted a hand. "I don't even remember going to any—" Abruptly, he snapped his mouth shut. Thumb and forefinger came up to press against his eyelids. "I went to a wedding in Michigan," he pushed through gritted teeth. "For a cousin. That's the picture you saw. I have no idea who the girl was. Probably a distant relative."

He faced front again.

The next time Izzy tried to swallow, she felt as if she were swallowing glass. What had his mother said when brandishing that photo? *"Does he look like a boy who's thinking about becoming a father with the girl he dated one summer after high school?"* She didn't clearly state that he had a new girlfriend, but that had been the implication. Hadn't it? Izzy closed her eyes and shook her head. It was all so long ago now.

She reopened her eyes when the ignition roared to life again. Glancing at Nate, she saw his profile, looking as if it had been carved on the side of a ridge, rock hard and unyielding.

The only sound on the hour-long ride home was the rumble of the BMW's motor and the roar of the tension between its passengers.

I have a son. A teenager.

Fists buried in the pockets of a lightweight hoodie he didn't really need, Nate strode through the streets of Thunder Ridge at two in the morning, his head covered and his eyes downcast, as if he were a teen himself.

He couldn't sleep. Hadn't even tried, actually. *I have a son I've never seen. Never even knew about.*

Eli.

The entire ride home, he had wondered whether Izzy would have told him about Eli at all if they hadn't run into the other boy. Nate couldn't remember the kid's name now, probably wouldn't recognize him if he was standing right before him. Once he'd realized Izzy had a son, *his* son, everything else had gone blurry.

Just before he'd dropped her at her house, Izzy had asked him whether he wanted her to tell him about Eli. He'd said, "Not now." He wouldn't have heard anything—there were too many thoughts, too many questions and accusations running through his brain. Now he felt guilty. Being a father—wasn't that about being present all the time, even when you didn't think you could be?

Being a father.

What did he know about that? Nothing.

Fury and resentment swelled inside him again. He couldn't deny Izzy's claim that he hadn't wanted to be a father at eighteen. But he'd actually thought about coming home, being responsible, until he'd heard about the miscarriage.

His fists balled tighter.

He couldn't even wrap his brain around being misinformed that Izzy had had a miscarriage. He'd wanted to phone his mother immediately last night, but in that moment he was too angry, his thoughts too accusatory to be of any service. There would be time enough to ask her why she'd shown the photo of the wedding to Izzy. He remembered now that he'd mailed it to his parents, since they hadn't been able to be there.

His shoes ate up the pavement, pace increasing with the rise of his anger. He walked until he reached town, and when the moonlight filtering through the trees turned to the light of streetlamps and twinkle lights that were never doused, the reality of his situation hit harder than ever before.

There's The General Store. Eli and Izzy have gone there for ice cream. When Jax's dad owned the place, he gave a free birthday scoop. *I don't know what flavor my son would choose.* Taking his hands from his pockets, he smacked a fist into the opposite palm.

Nate passed the bank. When he was a kid, they had "squirrel" accounts for elementary school students. Had Izzy walked Eli into the bank hand in hand to open his first account? Had Eli felt grown-up and important?

Lightning Hardware. First tool belt. Did Eli know the proper way to hammer a nail?

I've missed everything. Damn her. Damn them all.

Nate felt powerless in a way he'd never felt before in his life. The desire to smash the hardware store window and watch his reflection shatter into tiny, murderous shards was almost overpowering.

And then he saw another reflection, a patrol car pulling slowly along the curb. When Izzy's sheriff friend emerged from the car and sauntered over like Wild Bill Hickok on a posse hunt, Nate pivoted, spoiling for a fight.

"I've known Izz twelve years."

That was what the sonovabitch had boasted. Twelve years with Izzy and with *Nate's son.*

"It's a little late to go window-shopping," the sheriff drawled as he stepped onto the curb.

"I don't recall Thunder Ridge having a curfew." Nate heard the belligerence in his own tone. *Did you help my kid build his first birdhouse? Did you dress up like Santa Claus when he was five?*

"Well, you've been gone a long time. There's probably a lot of things you don't remember. Like the fact that we don't keep big-city hours."

"How do you know how long I've been gone?" *Did you toss him his first football?* "Is business so slow that you have time to check up on everyone who rolls into town?"

There was a sneer embedded in the question. The sheriff bristled.

"I forgot your name," Nate said, "and Izzy hasn't mentioned it in all the times we've been together. What is it?" *Yeah, take that, you rat bastard.*

"Sheriff Neel," came the deliberate reply.

"Sheriff Neel. So, what's that? Your first name? Like 'Hey, kids, Sheriff Neel is here to teach us about bike safety.' Or 'Look, folks, Sheriff Neel brought his ferret to show everyone how friendly the law is in Thunder Ridge.'"

At that moment, the law looked anything but friendly. "I'd like you to walk a straight line for me. Step over here." He pointed toward the edge of the curb.

Nate took a step, but forward, toward the sheriff, not toward where he pointed. "Haven't had a drop of alcohol in days."

"I didn't ask you that." Snapping his words into precise pieces, the sheriff ordered again, "Step over there."

Again Nate stepped forward. "No."

That did it. The sheriff began to take this more personally, as Nate intended. His anger roared to life, like turning on a gas fireplace. "Listen real careful, golden boy. You may have been used to getting whatever you wanted last time you were in Thunder Ridge, but it isn't going to work that way this go around. You screw with me or upset Izzy in any way, and I'll throw your self-important ass in a jail cell and forget where I put the key."

Sheriff Neel made every point by stabbing his finger in the direction of Nate's chest.

"Or," Nate said, baring his teeth, "you get it through your head that I'm not going anywhere. And when it comes to Izzy and *my son*—" Nate shoved a finger at the sheriff, making contact with the man's shoulder "—mind your own damn business."

Jaw clenched, Neel growled through his teeth, "Step back and keep your hands to yourself."

Like an eight-year-old goading a sibling on a car ride that had lasted too long, Nate stayed right where he was, keeping his finger aimed at the other man. "Maybe that's what you should have done. Kept your hands to yourself. Get your own family instead of pretending with somebody else's."

Self-control whooshed from the sheriff like air from a blown-out tire. "You dumbass," he said. "*I'm* pretending? Where the hell have you been? What family did you create? Obviously, you know about Eli, so the only words that ought to be coming out of your mouth are *thank you for stepping in when I was too selfish or indifferent to give a crap that I got a girl pregnant and*—"

The remainder of his dressing-down was lost as Nate's fist connected with Sheriff Neel's mouth. It didn't take but a second for the larger man to strike back with a punishing sock to the gut and then an attempt—but only an attempt, Nate was later proud to remember—to pull Nate's arms behind his back.

The next minute was filled with the men circling each

other, getting in as many shots as they could, spitting both blood and accusations and generally behaving in a fashion that would later make them supremely grateful they were having this fight at two in the morning on a deserted street.

Rocky road brownies, banana cream pie, four-cheese lasagna, Texas chili and corn bread, meat loaf… Biting her thumbnail, Izzy surveyed the buffet spread across her kitchen counter or bubbling on the stove and wondered what else she could make.

"Lemon-blueberry mousse." She headed to the pantry. Eli loved her lemon mousse. Light, fluffy and sweet-tart with tiny local blueberries, it would be just the thing to welcome him home from camp the day after tomorrow. Along, of course, with all the other Eli favorites she'd been making almost since she walked in the door last night.

She wasn't kidding herself. She knew teenage boys were different from PMS-ing women, who could be distracted by clever culinary maneuvers. Cooking gave her something to do with her nerves.

Exhausted, she piled ingredients onto the tiny slivers of counter space that remained. Even Latke, who typically stood by to gobble any morsel that fell to the floor when Izzy was cooking, had trudged off to her dog bed hours ago. The kitchen was a shambles, and so were Izzy's emotions.

Where did she stand with Nate? She had no idea. All she knew was that at two, no—she glanced at the kitchen clock—two *forty* in the morning, fear seemed more real than comfort.

Nate hadn't wanted to talk, hadn't wanted to listen, either. All she could do was wait for his next move. Clearly, they were not going to be bosom buddies, conferring lovingly on all things Eli. Not yet, at any rate.

"I'm going to go to bed. I am," she muttered to herself.

She already had enough food for Eli and Trey and a bunch of their friends. And other than identifying fear, she couldn't make heads or tails of how she was feeling.

Guilty? *Yes, darn it.*

Angry? *Well, yeah, sort of.* She hadn't cornered the market on bad decisions in this scenario, after all. Nate and his parents had a few bozo moves on their balance sheet, too. She swiped at a dusting of flour on the sink tiles.

Put the food away and go to bed, even if you don't sleep. Her nighttime thoughts were rarely clear and even more rarely helpful.

When the doorbell rang, she nearly dropped several pounds of lasagna.

Abandoning the glass pan in the kitchen, she hustled to the living room, her imagination already conjuring disastrous news about Henry or Sam or—

When she looked through the peephole and saw Derek, her heart turned over. *Eli.*

Flicking on the porch light and yanking open the door, she began to pepper him with questions. "What happened? Why were you called? Where is— Oh, my God." She peered closely at Derek's face, then exclaimed, "What happened to you? Your eye is—"

"Not as bad as his." Derek jerked his thumb toward the right. Nate stood on the porch, too, one eye almost completely shut, a cut on his cheek and several buttons ripped off his shirt. And he was handcuffed.

Izzy's jaw fell at the sight. She looked at Derek. "Why is he—"

"May we come in?" Derek's tone dripped sarcasm.

She backed up. Derek entered, followed by Nate, who looked angry enough to kill something once the handcuffs were removed.

Derek sniffed the air. "You baking?"

She nodded.

"So we didn't wake you up."

"No."

"Good." He jerked his head toward Nate. "Your friend has a bad temper."

Nate's injured eye started to pop open. He winced. "*I* have a bad temper? Look who's talking."

"Unless you want me to take you to a cell, shut it."

"Sure, take me to jail. It'll give me a chance to work on the police brutality charge I'm planning to file."

"Listen, you jackass—"

"Stop!" Izzy insisted, her nerves already raw. "You both have cuts that ought to be looked at." All she had on hand was antiseptic and a selection of drugstore bandages. No gauze or tape or anything. "I think you might need stitches," she told Nate.

"No, I don't," came the instantaneous, belligerent reply.

He lurched forward, shoved from behind. "Be polite," Derek growled.

"Derek," Izzy protested. Nate objected more colorfully to the push. "Will someone tell me what is going on here, please?"

"I found him loitering in front of the hardware store."

"Loitering," Nate scoffed, shaking his head.

"I said, shut it," Derek ordered.

"Up yours."

"Oh, for heaven's sake." Izzy went to get bandages while the men argued in her living room. She had never known Nate to get into a fight; nor had she ever heard him speak so rudely.

As for Derek, he had a distant history of getting into trouble but had been a veritable Boy Scout for nearly two decades. He even corrected Eli if her son used the word *stupid*.

Returning to the living room with bandages and disinfectant, she found Nate and Derek seated on her sofa, surly expressions on each of their bruised faces. Nate sat with his cuffed hands folded tensely on his lap.

"Derek, take the handcuffs off," Izzy requested.

"When I'm assured *your friend* can keep his hands to himself and after I've decided whether he needs to visit the jail for a spell or can be released on his own recognizance."

Nate rolled his eyes. "As if you know what *recognizance* means."

"And away we go," Derek said, reaching for Nate's arm.

"All right, obviously we are all in the midst of a tense situation," Izzy interjected.

Derek snorted. "Tense?"

"Can you define *tense* for him, too?" Nate suggested.

Derek growled, "How about we define *contempt for the law*, you arrogant—"

"That's enough, both of you!" Izzy set the first-aid items down *hard* on the coffee table. It was difficult to believe these were the rational men she'd loved.

"Derek," she said, "Nate just found out that Eli is his son. Obviously, he's feeling conflicted, at odds—"

"I know what *conflicted* means," Derek bit off.

"I know you do. And I'm sure you're feeling—" she almost said *vulnerable*, but neither of them was going to cop to that right now "—a lot of things, as well. You're involved in Eli's life—this affects you."

It was impossible to miss the resentment that filled Nate's expression.

"It's not going to be easy for any of us to figure out the new normal," she said, "but we have to, for Eli's sake. Whatever happened before now, whatever any one of us is feeling, Eli's needs have to come first. Can we agree on that?" When neither man spoke immediately, she put her hands on her hips. "Because if we can't, you are both welcome to leave. I mean it. History or no history. Future or no future."

The reprimand silenced them both. She pointed to Nate's hands. "Uncuff him." Derek released Nate and Nate rubbed his wrists. The requested silence reigned, highlighting the intense awkwardness of the situation. Whom, Izzy wondered, should she give first aid to first?

"Coffee? Tea? Lasagna?" she asked. Nobody answered and nobody smiled.

Derek stood. "I'm on duty."

Okay, Derek first. "I'll look at that cut on your face before you go."

"I'm fine." He headed to the door.

Oh, man, how long before they would be normal with each other again? Izzy followed him. "Derek," she said softly as he stepped onto the porch, "nothing will change between you and Eli, or you and me."

His mouth worked as if he wanted to say something, but in the end, his lips pressed into a thin smile. "Night, Izzy."

She remained on the porch until the squad car's headlights came on and Derek pulled away from the curb. Sad and confused about how to handle any of this, Izzy went back inside and shut the door.

Alone again with Nate.

Chapter Fourteen

Sitting on the couch, in Derek's vacated spot, Izzy soaked a cotton ball in antiseptic and touched it to Nate's forehead, slapping his hand when he tried to push the cotton away.

"If you're man enough to fight, you're man enough to suffer the consequences." When he looked at her, surprised by her matter-of-fact attitude to his injuries, she added quietly, "That's what I would tell Eli."

Nate was quiet for a moment. "Has he ever gotten into a fight?"

"Once." She continued to work on him as she shared the first of many stories she would likely tell him about his son. "He was eight, just finishing the second grade. He's always loved school, but that year was particularly hard for him because Reid Stoltz, who'd been his best friend since preschool, decided he couldn't play with Eli anymore. And he was very clear about why."

Nate's right brow rose above his swollen eye. "Why?"

This, Izzy realized, was one of the things she'd felt so

much trepidation about telling him. Shaking her head at her own faintheartedness, she forged ahead. "By third grade, the kids in Eli's class were starting to notice and care about who was 'different' and who was 'normal.' Reid decided he wanted a normal friend."

She reached up to put a bandage on the cut above Nate's eyebrow, but he stopped her.

"Explain that." He was watching her intently.

Izzy looked Nate straight in the eye. "Eli is deaf. He has assistive technology that helps him perceive some sounds, and an interpreter to help him in school, and he does really well. A's and B's in all his subjects. But in the schools he's gone to, he's always been the only kid with a serious hearing impairment. He stands out. That was especially tough when he was younger."

If Izzy was honest with herself, she'd been wondering for years how Nate would react to the news that his child was deaf. She noticed everything now—the lowering of his brow, the clouding over of his expression as questions raced through his mind. She saw him swallow. And then the question she realized she'd been dreading for over a decade:

"Was he born deaf?"

Izzy had worked through the guilt and the if-only's a long time ago. Such thoughts were useless in helping Eli move forward, so she'd relegated them to the late-night hours. She'd known, though, perhaps instinctively, that if Nate ever asked that question, the shadowy feelings would return.

"No. His hearing was normal." Rising from the sofa, she crossed to a bookcase, where several large photo albums nestled side by side. Pulling one off the shelf, she resumed her seat and opened it on her lap.

"This is Eli at a year and a half. He'd been toddling around for a few months already. He went on his first pony ride and loved it. And this—" she pointed to another photo "—is when we went berry picking on Sauvie Island. He ate so many blueberries his tongue was purple for hours."

Nate looked hungrier for the sight of his son than Eli had been for the berries. The certain knowledge that he had no intention of walking away without meeting Eli settled on her. And if he met Eli, he would want to remain part of his life; she knew it. The awareness was a relief and a worry.

"We lived in Portland his first couple of years. I got my GED, then worked as a waitress and took classes at Portland Community College."

Nate lifted his eyes from the photos to her. "And took care of a baby. That was a helluva lot on your shoulders."

She smiled. "Apparently, shoulders have a lot of muscle. The more you use them, the stronger they get."

Nate did not smile. "It was hard going."

"Some times were harder than others. I moved to Portland while I was pregnant. I lived with a friend of Henry's, who got me a job at a preschool that was in the office building where she worked. It was a perfect job, except I seemed to catch every bug the kids brought in. When Eli got sick the fall after we picked the berries, the diagnosis was congenital CMV. It's a virus I caught at the preschool and probably passed on to him while I was pregnant. No one knows exactly what happened, but the speculation is that his immune system fought it until he was twenty months. Then the virus began to manifest, and over a few months' time, he stopped talking, stopped responding the way he had been. He used to react to everything. There was nothing anyone could do. When he was two, he had almost total hearing loss."

Pain tightened Nate's features. "That must have scared the crap out of you."

She nodded. "Yes. Yes, it did." At one point, she had barely slept for two weeks. There was no point, however, in telling him that. She'd have given anything to have a hand to hold at night, someone who grieved as much as she that Eli could no longer hear a blue jay announce the dawn. There were people who had cared, but no one who'd shared the parenting moments with her.

"For a long time," she confessed, "I blamed myself. I even wondered if other people would blame me." She flapped a hand. "You know—idiotic teenage mother didn't know how to keep her baby safe. And if I messed up so early in his life, how on earth was I going to get through the rest of his childhood? There was one particularly bleak night when I even told myself I should have gone through with the adoption plans, because then I wouldn't have worked at the preschool and maybe he'd never have gotten sick."

He took her hand and squeezed hard. "You know that's not true."

She nodded. "Yes, I do know." But it was good…it was very, very good…to have Nate tell her, his eyes intent and sincere, his hand warm and strong around hers. If they had stayed together, if he had wanted to become a parent with her, those shoulders would have carried half the worries. "I don't know why I'm telling you this," she murmured, "except that I've never said it out loud before."

The photo album was lying across both their laps now, half on her left thigh and half on his right. Their clasped hands rested on top of a photo of Eli sitting on the back of a giant stuffed lion she'd found at a yard sale.

"How did you make your way back to Thunder Ridge?" Nate asked.

"I was still living with Joanne, Henry's friend, but she was getting ready to retire and planned to move in with her sister in Idaho. I was too busy and too stressed to make plans to find my own place. Henry and Sam cleaned out a room in their house and gave me my old job back with an offer to make me the manager as soon as I felt I could take on the extra responsibilities. So I came back and got a job and a place to live and babysitters. Lots of babysitters. All their support freed me up to advocate for Eli in every way I could."

The hand holding hers tightened again. "You were a rock star." His voice was rough, ragged. He meant it.

"How do you know?" she asked softly.

He raised their hands. His lips touched her knuckles. "I know, because I know you. I know—" He swallowed heavily. "I know you said yes when I said no. Thank you for doing that. Thank you for raising our son."

She nodded *you're welcome*. Hope kindled, hope that he was not going to view Eli as damaged, but simply unique.

The moment of connection between them was profound and bittersweet. It was the moment they might have shared in the hospital as they marveled at the brand-new life they'd taken part in creating. Over the top of their baby's head, they would have held gazes as they were doing now. And they would have kissed.

Their faces were so close it wouldn't have taken more than an accident for their lips to touch. Someone must have moved back, though—Izzy wasn't sure whether it was she or Nate—because the moment of soul-aching intimacy ended with a spurt, not a spark.

Gently Nate released Izzy's hand so that it rested again on the scrapbook. Then he ran his free hand through his hair and asked, "How does Eli communicate? How will I talk to him?"

How will I, not *if I.* And so they moved into a new phase of their relationship: an informed truce.

She explained about the cochlear implant Eli had at age eleven and about how frightening the change had been, even though they had welcomed it.

"I want to get to know him before he finds out I'm his

father." Nate appeared to be deep in thought as he said this. "I want to be able to ask him questions, get the answers without filters."

"Okay. I understand wanting to get to know him without the pressure of trying hard to make it work. But I don't think we should wait too long. Teenagers really don't like secrets, unless they're the ones keeping them."

Nate nodded. "A couple of meetings. Can you help me learn to sign language?" He looked at her with such open need, like a brand-new father asking how to hold the baby.

Working as a team, they strategized how to introduce Eli to Nate, and Izzy taught Nate a couple of super simple signs and the finger alphabet. As they pored over the scrapbook together, she signed as well as spoke her descriptions of the photos.

"It's beautiful," he said, sitting back at one point and simply staring at her.

She'd just signed and said, "I love Eli's face in this photo."

Nodding at his compliment, she murmured, "I know. He has a perfect nose, doesn't he?"

"I meant the signing," Nate said, sipping the coffee she'd made. "The way your hands move—it's beautiful. I like watching you."

She blushed, but happily. "You don't *have* to use ASL, you know. He can hear decently now, and when he can't understand something, he reads lips. It's still hard for people who don't know him well to understand his speech, and I think it's easier for him to sign certain things. Plus, signing is his first language, really. That's a hard thing to give up."

"I'll learn it. I want to."

Izzy stared. Finally, she whispered, "I was scared." It was a discovery as much as an admission, which Nate seemed to understand, because he waited while she gathered her thoughts. "There have been times…like when he went into surgery for the implant…that I wanted to phone you. I wanted to tell you about Eli so badly, even if you decided not to pursue a relationship with him. But I was too scared."

He nodded, looking down at his clasped hands. "Okay. I'm trying to understand that. You didn't know how I'd react, I could have walked away again… I'm trying to understand all that, but it's hard, damn it. It's hard to accept your reasons—anyone's reasons—for not telling me."

She nodded, knowing she couldn't change how he felt, that it wasn't even her right. But truth was important, so she continued, "That's not the only thing I was afraid of. With Eli, I had a family for the first time. Real family. I didn't want to lose it."

He looked surprised.

"I was selfish," she admitted. "What if you or your parents did change your minds and wanted Eli in your lives?" She stopped short of adding *and you didn't want me*. She didn't have to say it. "I didn't want to share. I didn't want to lose him." Her voice cracked, even though she was less afraid now, because she trusted that Nate wasn't going to take Eli away. She was still afraid, however, of the changes in store. "It was wrong of me. I should have told you I kept him. I *am* sorry."

Lowering his head, Nate covered his face with his hands, then pushed them through his hair. "Me, too. You're not the only one who was scared. I couldn't imagine any future but the one I already had planned. I'm sorry I walked away and sorry my parents lied. You deserved better. You deserved a hell of a lot better."

"Well, that future of yours looked pretty darn good, even from the cheap seats." She gave him a smile tinged with self-deprecating humor. "I don't like that your parents lied, but if Eli became a father at eighteen…" She took a deep breath, blowing it out hard. "I'd probably think I knew what was best. Maybe I'd even let the end justify the means."

She closed the scrapbook they'd been looking at and set it atop the two others on the coffee table. "I've certainly been playing God with Eli's life and yours and mine." Her smile turned weary. "I'm willing to stop."

"What do you mean?"

What *did* she mean?

Looking at Nate the man was superior, she realized, to looking at Nate the boy. Sheer physical beauty had turned into something more complex, as if he'd been broken and put back together again even better. A little rougher around the edges, a little battered in spots that had once been perfect. But through those worn bits, she could see his soul, and it looked good.

"I mean I trust the right thing to happen if I let go. And by letting go," she hastened to add, "I do not mean you can take him to Chicago with you tomorrow. I'm just saying it's time to be honest and to see where it takes us. See where it takes you and Eli. And me."

Nate leaned toward her, his eyes at once sober with gratitude and shining with anticipation. "If he's anything like you, I'm a lucky man."

Izzy tried to ignore the knocking of her heart and the way her gaze seemed to want to fasten on his lips. She cleared her throat. "Eli will be home the day after tomorrow. Come to dinner on Friday?"

"Absolutely."

Chapter Fifteen

"Who's this guy?"

Since he'd returned from camp, Eli had been using his voice more than his hands to speak. Izzy thought her son had grown an inch also, but that could have been her imagination. Eli seemed to have matured in the two weeks he'd been away. Now, as they stood in the kitchen, assembling ingredients for the "monster burritos" that were her son's favorite meal, Izzy's stomach buzzed with nerves.

"I told you, honey, he's an old friend, and he'd like to meet you."

"He's the dude Trey saw you with at the zoo?"

"Yes."

Pausing in his cheese grating, Eli popped a hunk of the cheddar into his mouth. "Mom. You're dating."

"No! I'm not." Pushing her loose hair behind her ear, she chopped an onion, taking care to look up so Eli could assist his own hearing by reading her lips while she spoke. "Eli, don't try to read anything into this, okay? Just enjoy getting to know him. I think you'll like Nate."

"Do *you* like Nate?"

Affecting an innocent look, the fourteen-year-old continued to eat rather than grate cheese. He wasn't used to her spending time with unfamiliar men, Izzy reminded herself, and that was why he was probing. She hadn't dated anyone in a hundred years. Slicing the onion with perhaps a little more vigor than necessary, she responded as if it should be obvious, "Why would I introduce you to someone I *don't* like? Can you please grate at least the same amount of cheese you're scarfing?"

Eli grinned. And shoved several tortilla chips into his mouth at once before resuming his duties.

The soothing sounds of chopping and grating lulled Izzy for the moment while she pondered again the wisdom of having Eli meet Nate before explaining who Nate was. They really didn't look that much alike. Eli wasn't going to guess, at least not tonight. And Nate had confirmed earlier today that he wanted time to "get Eli to like me" before they told him the truth. Nate still seemed so nervous about it that Izzy had agreed. But she was worried. There had already been too many secrets.

It'll be okay. It will, she reassured herself. Nate was likable and very cool. At least, he seemed like the type of person a teenage boy would find cool. She was making far too big an issue of *when* they told him; really, they should probably focus on *how*. And if she thought she was nervous tonight, she could only imagine how Nate was feeling—

"So, Mom, do you *like* him like him?"

"Oh, my gosh, Eli!" Izzy nearly sliced her finger off with the knife. The question sent her heart rate into orbit. "Can we just please— Let's concentrate on making dinner, 'cause we're running late. What kind of olives do you want for the burritos? Black or the green kind with pimentos?"

Wiping his hands, Eli pulled his phone from his back pocket and began thumb-typing.

Izzy swatted him with a dish towel so he'd look at her. "What are you doing?"

"Texting Trey to tell him he's right." Eli laughed, thoroughly enjoying himself, and Izzy realized with no small amount of surprise that her son was truly fine with the idea that his mother might want to date.

The sound of the doorbell, along with the flashing chime they'd had since before Eli's cochlear implant, precluded further conversation.

Izzy raced to the sink to wash her hands.

"I'll get it," Eli announced, still laughing as he sped from the kitchen with the clear intention of beating her to the door. Izzy had to stop herself from turning off the water with soap still on her hands. She'd already promised herself several times that she would let this meeting and all subsequent meetings between father and son unfold without her interference. Man, it was hard. Bracing her hands on the edge of the sink, she counted her breaths. *Let them do this on their own. Trust.*

On the other hand, there would never be another first meeting between father and son. She should get a picture. *Or, at the very least, watch it so I can describe it back to them at a later date.*

To get to the living room, she had to hurdle over Latke, who was taking a rest stop in the hallway. Izzy skidded to a stop as Eli swung the door wide and said in his nasal monotone, "Hi. I'm Eli. Are you Nate? My mom is in the kitchen. Come on in."

Nate seemed to be frozen on the threshold. Izzy held her breath.

Hungry eyed, Nate stared at her son…his son…their son…with an expression approaching awe. She could see him absorbing every detail—fair skin tanned a light gold, hair the color of an oak leaf in autumn, his mother's eyes, all ten fingers, the legs of a colt, feet encased in a serious pair of sneakers.

Nate stuck out his hand. Izzy understood instantly that the gesture was not about good manners. *He wants to touch.*

She was gratified that her lessons on etiquette had not gone completely unheeded. Grasping Nate's hand, Eli pumped it heartily.

Nate, clearly, could have continued standing there, shaking hands indefinitely. It was Eli who eventually dropped the hold and said, just in case Nate hadn't heard the first time, "You can come in."

"Hi!" she called brightly, acting as if she'd just come around the corner. "Glad you could make it, Nate. Come into the kitchen. We're just putting the finishing touches on dinner. We're having monster burritos, Eli's favorite. You can help me grate some cheese. Eli keeps eating it all. Eli—" she backhanded Eli lightly on the arm as they passed "—pour Nate an iced tea, would you, please? We'll sit down to eat in a little while."

Okay, so much for allowing the evening to unfold without her interference. But the evening did improve from there.

As they sat down at the table to eat, Nate asked Eli what his favorite subject was in school.

"We're learning about the Renaissance," Eli answered. "My class is making models of the Capitoline Museums."

Nate's eyes lit up like sparklers. "Italy is on my bucket list."

Eli nodded. "Mine, too."

Izzy hadn't even known her son had a bucket list! "What are the Capitoline Museums?" she asked.

Both Eli and Nate looked at her, their expressions so alike that her breath caught at the similarity.

"Mom, seriously? You went to high school, right?"

"Yes, smart aleck, and I'm quite sure the Capitoline Museums were not mentioned."

Eli looked at Nate. "Where did you go to high school?"

As their son worked on a too-big bite of burrito, Nate and Izzy shared a sharp glance. "Right here," Nate answered. "Same high school you're at."

"Is that where you met my mom?"

Izzy's appetite vanished. Was this where the whole truth would emerge or more lies would be told?

"Yes." Wiping his mouth with one of the cloth napkins Izzy had laid out, Nate sat back. "Your mother was a grade behind me."

Eli looked between them, a broad grin taking over his face. "What was she like?" Izzy opened her mouth to redirect the conversation, but Eli held out a hand. "You don't get to answer this, Mom."

Izzy's heart gave her ribs a pounding as Nate considered his response.

"She was…very much the way she is now. Sincere. A hard worker. Serious."

"Kinda boring, Mom," Eli teased.

Nate smiled. "She was also loyal and giving. And brave." He looked directly at Izzy. "One of the bravest people I know." He returned his gaze to Eli. "She'd walk through fire for you."

Though he kept his tone light, he left no doubt that he meant every word. Izzy's heart settled into a sweet, soft thud.

"So, Italy is on your bucket list, hmm?" she said to Eli, heaping tortilla chips onto his plate. "First I've heard of it."

"I want to do a year of college there. I thought I'd wait to break the news to you." He glanced at Nate. "She gets kinda emotional and writes a lot of lists when I leave Thunder Ridge. Not really looking forward to the scene when I leave the country."

"I am very supportive of your independence," Izzy protested, tearing up at the mere thought of her son, her baby, living an ocean away.

With the conversation safely deflected from questions about her and Nate, Izzy settled back and watched the two men she'd loved the most in her life. They discussed architecture and the Trail Blazers, the merits of kayaking versus paddleboarding (kayaking won by a mile), and why they loved the TV show *Grimm*. Izzy shuddered.

When Eli switched from spoken language to ASL, which he did unconsciously sometimes when addressing her, Nate simply looked to Izzy for translation.

Shooing them back to their seats as they rose to help her ferry the dinner plates to the kitchen, she met Nate's eyes above Eli's head. *Thank you*, he mouthed.

And when she returned a few minutes later with pound cake and fresh peach ice cream, Nate looked up again as Eli was teaching him how to play Geometry Dash on his phone and this time mouthed, *He's fantastic.*

Altogether, Nate stayed three and a half hours. Eli said he was still recovering from two weeks with younger kids and that he was ready for bed, so Izzy walked Nate to his car.

It occurred to her as she closed the front door and stepped into the evening that for the first time in Eli's fourteen years, she could discuss her boy with the only other person likely to be as proud of his every burp as she'd always been.

Nate had eaten at Michelin star restaurants, conversed with CEOs and foreign investors over Kobe-steak crostini and bottles of wine worth four hundred dollars. But he knew he would forever think of this as the best night of his life.

Beneath a lavender sky that was deepening rapidly now

to purple, Izzy walked beside him, dressed in another of her simple sundresses, with skinny straps and a formfitting top that showed her figure hadn't changed much since she was seventeen. It was easy to imagine, just for a moment, that they'd stayed together, that his life was right here where stars, not streetlamps or skyscrapers, lit the night, and where "Good night, son" and "I love you, Isabelle" could have been the last words he said every night.

Common sense tried to tell him he was reacting to the big emotions of the night, nothing more. He glanced down at Izzy, her silky hair brushing her bare shoulders, her feet small and pretty in simple sandals, and he thought, *How could I not love her for what she's given me?* The delicate-looking woman beside him had more strength in her pinkie than he had in his entire body. Real strength. The kind that mattered. He owed her more than he could ever repay.

Turning toward her as they reached his rental car, she said, "It was a good night. A great start, I thought. Eli really likes you."

Hope and pleasure swelled inside him. "Think so?"

"Oh, yeah. You had him at Trail Blazers." Her impish smile shot straight to his heart.

"He's the luckiest kid in the world to have you for a mother."

She blinked, temporarily lost for words. "I've stumbled a lot," she said at last, shrugging. "I just keep loving him."

He nodded. "Like I said, lucky kid. I wouldn't have been half the parent you've been."

"That's not true."

"It is. You knew yourself, Izzy. Even at seventeen."

"Me?" She shook her head. "No. Being Eli's parent has taught me all sorts of things I didn't know I needed to learn. That will happen to you, too."

His throat felt thick. She was speaking as if she accepted

that he would be an ongoing presence in Eli's life. "I meant it when I said you were brave."

She nodded. "I know you meant it. Thank you."

Pressing his thumb and forefinger to the inner corner of his welling eyes, he admitted, "I was pretty damn scared Eli wasn't going to like me at all."

Compassion transformed her face. "Well. What's not to like?" A moment passed, and she said quietly, "Good night, Nate."

He didn't want to end this night, not by a long shot, but it was getting late, and she probably had to get up early the next day. As for himself, he wasn't going to sleep a wink.

Afraid to touch her, knowing that if he did, he wouldn't be able to let her go, Nate settled for drinking in one long last moment with the mother of his son, before he said, "Good night, Isabelle."

Izzy turned from Nate with conflict pulsing through her veins. She couldn't wait to get back to the house, to talk to Eli if he was still up and to debrief with herself, too. On the other hand, leaving Nate tonight felt as hard as it had been when she was seventeen and leaving him meant returning to a lonely, miserable trailer.

She'd seen new expressions on his face tonight, expressions she was willing to bet that no one but she had ever witnessed. Enjoying their child together had been holy. Magical. And then there had been the moment by the car when she'd thought…sensed, really…was almost *certain*, in fact…that he was going to kiss her again.

But he didn't.

And, let's face it, almost kissing someone didn't count for much of anything. It wasn't worth thinking about. Anyway, she knew she couldn't kiss him anymore. That would be insanity. The very definition of *irresponsible*. Utter emotional suicide, and he surely realized that, too.

All these thoughts Izzy managed to pack into the two steps she took away from Nate.

Before the third step, she felt his fingers clamp around her left wrist. Taking her by surprise, he turned her around and pulled her back to him, and before she could even wonder what to expect, his lips were on hers.

Warm. Firm. Hungry but gentle…exploring more than her mouth, exploring her feelings, too. A good kiss was more than foreplay; it was a conversation, and, oh wow, she could talk to Nate all night long.

His hands held her face, then moved into her hair. Her fingers curled into his chest, then slid up to his shoulders to delve into the hair at his nape. By the time he raised his head, Izzy was panting. Either she was seriously out of shape, or this kiss was aerobic.

She lowered her forehead to his chest, and Nate placed a lingering kiss on the top of her head, which was almost sweeter than his kissing her lips. Well, *as* sweet, anyway.

She shook her head. "Complications," she murmured.

Tucking a finger beneath her chin, he raised her face so he could see her. "What?"

"We shouldn't add complications to our situation."

He dropped a quick, soft peck beside her mouth. Teasing, she thought, and very erotic.

Endeavoring to keep her wits about her, she placed her palms on his chest to create a little space between them. "Every kid with estranged or missing-in-action parents has the same fantasy."

Breaching her space-creating efforts, he dropped another kiss, this time on her jaw. "Yeah?"

He wasn't listening. The barely there shadow of his stubble rubbed her chin. He felt so good. Smelled so good. "Yes," she murmured, closing her eyes, fingers gathering a fistful of his shirt. He felt so good. Smelled so good. "Every kid wants his estranged parents to get together again. But mostly that happens in the movies. In real life, it's so much more complicated, and when it doesn't work out, everyone is disappointed, and…" One of his hands was massaging the back of her head.

Letting go of his shirt, she thumped a fist against his pecs—excellent, rock-solid pecs. "Eli comes first," she said with more force as he nuzzled her ear, which sent goose bumps shivering up and down her arms *and* legs, then nipped her lobe with his teeth, a tiny, playful nibble. "If anything else we do could hurt him—"

She didn't have to finish that sentence.

Inhaling deeply, Nate pulled back, though he kept her in the circle of his arms.

"All right, I hear you. We should put first things first."

She nodded.

"We didn't do that last time," he acknowledged.

"No." She shook her head, feeling sad suddenly. "Cart before the horse, and all that."

"Yeah." His hands moved to the less intimate area of her upper arms. Lightly, he rubbed up and down, then gave her a squeeze and let go. The letting-go part was filled with palpable reluctance. "Okay," he said in a rough, trying-to-control-himself voice that was very flattering. "Job one—getting to know my son."

"Yes."

In the darkening night, he searched her face. "What happens in the movies…when the parents get back together?"

"They usually don't show anything beyond the reunion. Maybe it works for a while and then the couple part again and break their children's hearts."

"Cheery. Or they pull each other up every one of life's mountains and enjoy the view together for the rest of their lives."

Izzy wanted that so much it scared the stuffing out of her. "In a Disney movie. But who lives in a Disney movie?"

"No one," he agreed. "But almost every story is rooted in at least some truth." He reached out to tuck strands of her hair behind her ears, then brushed his knuckles down the side of her cheek. "So, I was a big Lewis Carroll fan as a kid. *Alice in Wonderland.* Go figure. You know what Alice says?"

She shook her head.

Nate's lips curved. "Something to the effect that she believes in up to six impossible things. Usually before breakfast."

Chapter Sixteen

Nate flew to Chicago for four days the following week for business and personal reasons. He took care of the business, then went to see his mother.

Lynette Thayer's Lincolnshire, Illinois, condominium was a world away from Nate's childhood home in Thunder Ridge. Back then, the Thayers had been strictly working-class, and their personal belongings had reflected that fact. Now a hutch filled with bone china and fine crystal graced one wall in the dining area, where Nate and his mother sat, awkwardly pushing Caesar salads around their plates.

"You knew," Nate said, his voice the only sound in the apartment, "you knew about Eli, didn't you?"

With her eyes on her lettuce, Lynette nodded slowly. Behind the designer glasses she favored these days, her small eyes blinked several times. "I've known for quite a few months now. I didn't know how to tell you. When your friend Jax called you about his project..."

Setting her fork on the edge of her plate, Lynette sighed.

Her hands, thin and heavily veined, folded resignedly in her lap. She spoke so softly Nate had to strain to catch the next words.

"I was frightened, but glad you were going back. I wanted to tell you years ago that we lied about Isabelle and the baby. But your father had his first heart attack, and then you met Julianne, and—" She sighed again. "Everything seemed so perfect between you two. We assumed Isabelle would put the baby up for adoption when she left town. I told myself it couldn't be good for anyone to dredge up the past."

Lynette looked at her son, and for once her carefully applied makeup was incapable of masking her age. She looked older than he'd ever seen her. "It's impossible to deceive another person unless we deceive ourselves first," she murmured. "I learned that lesson the hard way."

When her lower lip began to tremble, Nate could see his mother reach deep inside for the steely strength that was more typical of her.

"When I told you Isabelle miscarried the baby, I first had to convince myself that I was protecting your future rather than my desires for your future. I told myself that my life experience gave me the privilege to decide what was best. I robbed you of the only child you might ever have. And I let that girl…that young girl…deal with pregnancy and childbirth on her own."

Nate had expected a difficult conversation today. He had cautioned himself not to accuse or blame even though he'd wanted to shout and point fingers and demand an explanation he could accept. Now he knew there would be none of the above. No shouting, no chastising, no pound of flesh and no explanation that would ever make up for the years he'd missed with his son. The years they had all missed.

"Izzy managed well." He said it as matter-of-factly as he could. "Her bosses at the deli helped. She's a great mother."

Lynette nodded. "I hired a private detective to find the child after you and Julianne broke up. It didn't take him any time at all to locate Isabelle and…your son. He sent me photos." She looked at Nate, and this time she was incapable of stemming the tears that flowed down her cheeks. "I had no idea how to tell you. I'm proud of nothing I've done. But I hope now you'll be able to have some kind of relationship. Some sort of…"

Lynette hid her face behind her hands as sobs shook her body.

Nate didn't have to think or weigh his options. He moved to his mother's side and put his arms around her. In the past couple of months, he'd learned enough about human frailty and family to know they sometimes walked hand in hand.

"I think we all have enough regrets to fill an ocean," he said and felt her nod against his cheek. "I'm done with that. We start from here."

"Have you seen him, Nate? Does he know?"

"I've seen him. He's terrific. He doesn't know who I am yet."

"Oh, dear—"

"That'll come. I have pictures on my phone. You want to see?"

Sniffling into her napkin, Lynette looked at him with watery appreciation. "May I?"

While Nate was in Chicago, Izzy reflected that having him back in her life made it harder than ever to be away from him. Thankfully, approximately thirty hours after he left Thunder Ridge, he phoned, saying he missed her and Eli. Izzy felt happy, champagne-like bubbles popping in her chest. Then he said he was wrapping up some business and added, "I went to see my mother."

Instantly, trepidation turned the champagne bubbles into fizzing anxiety.

"She hired a private investigator and found out you and Eli were in Thunder Ridge. She's felt guilt ridden for years, but for a long time couldn't face admitting what she'd done and then didn't know how to tell me once she found you. When the job opportunity with Jax came up, she waited, hoping I'd discover everything for myself—admittedly not the best way to handle it, but I think it's accurate to say she was terrified."

Izzy put a hand to her temple. "This is hard to take in all at once. Did you tell her you met Eli?"

"I did. She cried. We don't have to decide anything now, you know, about visits or anything. She'd like to write to you, though, if you're okay with that, and apologize."

Izzy wasn't sure what she was okay with in this moment, but she agreed, nervous yet finally trusting that Nate would always protect their son's feelings. And hers.

Even though Nate had planned to be away four days, he didn't last that long. On day three, he returned. "Indefinitely," he responded when she asked how long he could stay.

She invited him to join her and Eli on a bike ride to Trillium Lake for a picnic. After they ate, Eli grinned knowingly, gave her broad winks and a thumbs-up behind Nate's back, then took off when he met two of his friends.

Nate was obviously disappointed he wasn't going to spend more time with his son. He glanced around at the families, tourists mostly, camping in the park and rowing or swimming or sunbathing on the lake. He seemed particularly interested in a young couple with a toddler. It was easy to follow the train of his thoughts, and Izzy experienced a stab of guilt that Nate and Eli had not been able to share a first swim and first canoe ride like the little family he was watching.

Feeling her guard lowering more and more where he was concerned, she told him how she felt.

"Let's take guilt off the table, okay?" he suggested. "I've had several big helpings already, and all I have to show for it is indigestion." Lying on his side on the blanket she'd brought, he squinted up at her. "It's probably too public here to kiss you, hmm?"

Pleasure colored her cheeks. "Probably."

"Yeah, and we have that agreement about not putting the cart before the horse."

"We do."

"I bought a canoe," he announced. "Big enough for three. Would you and Eli like to join me for a float on the lake tomorrow?"

Oh, boy, would she. But she donned her mother hat. "I have to work tomorrow. You should take Eli. Just the two of you." Nate looked excited and adorably nervous. She placed a hand on his arm, enjoying the role of reassuring him instead of the other way around. "He'll love it."

After half a day on the lake with his son—his *son*!— Nate was sure he'd found the missing link in his life. He couldn't get enough of looking at Eli, studying the boy the way one would study a painting by a master.

Nate was remembering, too, to look directly at Eli when speaking, and Eli's speech was becoming more accessible to him all the time. As they finished their lunches on the shore while their canoe bobbed in the water, Eli talked about his basketball coach's obvious hairpiece and about how one year, the team glued a toupee onto a basketball and some kid named Lyle dribbled the thing all the way up the court before the coach noticed.

Nate laughed, enjoying his son's delight in the retelling as much as he enjoyed the story.

"Do you want to take one more spin around the lake?"

he asked as he wrapped up the remains of the lunch Izzy had packed for them.

Izzy. Standing at her front door in jeans and a Pickle Jar T-shirt, with her hair in a simple ponytail and her face free from makeup, she'd looked utterly beautiful this morning. Standing with her and Eli on the front porch, Nate finally had the feeling for which he'd been searching nearly two decades: wholeness. He felt whole.

He had a surprise for Izzy, one he hoped would make his intentions for their combined futures very clear. But there were details to be hammered out, and he couldn't tell her for a couple of weeks.

"Yeah, let's go again," Eli agreed. "Straight across. We can beat our last time."

"Not much for relaxing paddles around the lake, are you?" Nate mock complained, but, really, he felt invigorated by his son's boundless energy.

Grinning, Eli jumped up to help pack the remains of the picnic so they could get into the water. As he began to fold the blanket they'd been sitting on, he asked, "So, you like my mom?"

The question was so unexpected Nate dropped a thermos of lemonade. He looked at his son, wondering how to play this. Sincere? Casual? Should he affect misunderstanding?

But Eli wasn't judging and didn't seem unhappy about the prospect. Nate answered honestly but carefully. "Yes, I like your mom. I like being around her. I like being around you, too."

Instantly, he regretted saying that to a teenage boy, but Eli didn't seem awkward or embarrassed.

"Okay." Nodding with more sophistication than he probably had, Eli advised, "You should keep seeing her, then. I think she likes you, too."

Nate would have loved to pursue that, but today was about Eli. He shoved the picnic items in a cooler, stowed everything under the bushes where they'd docked, and tossed out a challenge. "*Twice* across the lake. First time with only you rowing, and second with only me. We time it, and the winner buys root beer floats."

Eli's smile seemed to spread all the way across his face. "Triple-scoop waffle cones."

"Done."

They got in the canoe, and Eli worked tirelessly, muscles pumping while Nate timed him. He crowed with victory as they reached the bank.

"Not so fast," Nate said darkly, but he enjoyed his son's competitiveness. "My turn."

The sun was hot and high. Peeling his T-shirt over his head, Nate got down to business, grabbing the oars. Eli heckled him good-naturedly. Nate was grinning before he was halfway across the lake. By the time he'd reached the far bank, he was crowing victory, just to see Eli's reaction. It didn't occur to him until the race was over that Eli was no longer laughing. No longer even talking. Or smiling.

He didn't even want to argue over who'd won. "It doesn't matter," Eli mumbled, sullen. "It's late. I have to go."

No conversation was desired. Nate didn't have enough experience to know how to address the sudden mood shift. He tried joking. "If you demand a rematch, I guarantee I don't have enough energy to win."

"I don't want a rematch. I need to go."

The silence extended uncomfortably. "Eli, if I did something…or said something that bothered you…" Nate stopped, having no idea how to continue. "Do you want to talk about something?"

But Eli wasn't even looking at him. He was pretending, Nate was sure, that he didn't hear what was being said.

Fear, frustration and guilt—he wasn't sure over what— began to gnaw at Nate. By the time they got back to town, he was as grouchy as Eli.

Carrying the picnic gear to the house, he thought he might drop everything and run so he could return to the hotel and try to figure out what the hell he'd done wrong, but Izzy ushered them both in, saying she had a new dessert to try out on them. Something she wanted to start serving at the deli.

Eli hadn't wanted to get the ice cream, and he didn't want any dessert now.

He signed something to his mother. No talking so Nate could be included. He didn't even glance in Nate's direction.

Izzy frowned. She both signed and spoke, "You didn't tell me you were seeing Trey tonight. I made dinner. I thought we could all eat and watch *Hotel Transylvania*. Do you know Nate likes that movie as much as we do?"

Eli did glance in his direction then, with an expression that approached a sneer. He signed again to his mother.

"Why?" she asked. "Don't you feel well? And, honey, remember that Nate doesn't know ASL, so you need to speak, too."

"Fine. I said, if I can't go to Trey's, then I'm going to my room. Okay?"

"No," Izzy said, "not okay." She looked at Nate. "What happened? What's wrong?"

Her question seemed to incense Eli. "What are you asking him for? He's not part of this family. He doesn't know anything about me."

"Eli—"

"He's not! Who is he? Some guy you're dating? Or not even dating? You want me to call him 'Uncle Nate'?"

"Hey!" Nate waded in. "Don't talk to your mother that way."

Eli turned on him. "Don't tell me what to do. Who are you? My life isn't any of your business. Neither is hers." He gestured to his mother. "Why are you hanging around all of a sudden? *Who are you?*"

Izzy and Nate did probably the worst thing they could have done at that point: they stared mutely at their son.

Eli shook his head, mumbled, "Never mind. I don't care!" and raced up the stairs to his attic bedroom.

Thunderstruck, Izzy looked at Nate. "Does he know? Did you—"

"No, of course not, not without telling you. I don't know what happened. Everything seemed great, and then—"

"What?"

Nate spread his hands. "I don't know. It changed." He felt like an ass for having no better explanation.

Seeing his frustration, she put a hand on his arm. "Teenagers are like that sometimes," she attempted to reassure, but it was obvious she wasn't reassured herself. "I'm going to go up and talk to him."

"I'll—" he shrugged, feeling impotent "—head back to the hotel."

"No. I've got iced tea and coffee cake, and... Stay," she said, looking at him imploringly. "It's time we started working through some of these parenting things together." She tried a smile. "Lord knows we need the practice."

Nate wanted to hold her. He wanted to give her strength. And get some for himself. He wanted to know how to do this, right damn now.

"I'll go up and talk to him first," she suggested. "See if I can find out what's really bothering him. You'll wait?"

He nodded. "I'll wait." *As long as it takes.*

When Izzy walked into her son's room, Eli was on his bed, throwing his basketball far too close to the ceiling. Because of her own background, Izzy had taken numerous parenting classes at community college and tried to balance firmness with empathy, which was often easier said than done. At this moment, she opted for firmness. Stealing the basketball from midair before Eli could catch it again, she shot it at the laundry hamper and scored. "You," she told her son, using voice and hands, "were rude. What's going on?"

Deliberately, Eli stared at the ceiling, ignoring her.

She thumped him on the shoulder. "Hey. Don't do that. Talk to me. What is going on?"

Using ASL only, he signed. *Maybe you should tell me what's going on. Why don't* you *talk to* me? His hands stabbed the air as he spoke.

There was only one person in the world Izzy felt she knew as well as herself. When Eli turned twelve, she'd had to amend that to *almost* as well as herself, because like most tween brains, Eli's could be a complete mystery at times. But, still, she knew her son.

She tapped his thigh so he'd scoot over, but he refused. And then he looked at her. His eyes were so much like hers. As a baby and toddler, they'd looked at her with a trust that had made her heart feel ten times bigger than it was. As he'd gotten older, his eyes had held fear, anger, hurt— all the emotions it took to grow up. But never, never had he looked at her with the resentment and fury and mistrust she saw now.

"Who is he?" Eli clamped down on each word as if he were tearing off bites of the toughest beef jerky. "Is he the man who— Is…is he…my father?"

An earthquake rolled through Izzy's body. Eli put his arm over his eyes, blocking her out, but not before she saw the glisten of tears.

"Eli. My boy," she whispered, reaching for his arm. He jerked it away. "I'm sorry," she said.

You said you always tell me the truth. He continued to sign only, reverting to the language they knew best.

Lying on his bed, he looked so young and so knowing and so afraid. Izzy felt as if he'd lassoed her heart and was squeezing. "I know," she said sadly. "I've been too scared. You never asked me much about your father," she began haltingly. "Not telling you was the easy way out, and I took it."

I was afraid he was a jerk. I didn't want to know about him. I thought I'd hate him.

ASL was a beautiful language, and Izzy had often thought it was particularly beautiful when used to express strong anger or grief or love. Now, as she watched her son's eloquent hands, she felt his emotions.

He's got the same birthmark I do. Over his ribs. I saw it when he took off his shirt.

Izzy closed her eyes. Lord, she'd forgotten. Over the years, she'd actually forgotten that Nate shared the same uniquely shaped birthmark that decorated Eli's skin. Nate's, she recalled now, had been lighter, less noticeable.

She had to restrain her impulse to take her son in her arms. Deep inside he must have wondered, must have sensed Nate's presence was something more than just a friend getting to know him.

He's never been around before. Ever, Eli signed strongly. *Why is he here now? How come he changed his mind?*

"Changed his mind?"

About wanting a kid.

This was the hard part, the part that would reveal her weaknesses—and Nate's—as much as their strengths. This was the part she couldn't put a good spin on, but their son was demanding the truth, and he deserved it.

"We were so young. Not much older than you are now. We weren't mature enough to handle a long-term relationship, much less a pregnancy. Nate already had a scholarship to a great college…" As succinctly as she could, trying her best not to blame anyone, she explained that Nate's parents wanted him to continue on his path, and then gently, so gently, she revealed that they'd talked about making an adoption plan. The wounded surprise on her son's face nearly sliced her in two.

"I don't know if you'll understand this until you're the parent of a teenager yourself. Nate's parents understood what it takes to raise a child, and they didn't think we were ready."

But you *kept me.*

"I did. I was selfish." She wanted so badly to touch him, to comfort him. But he was still too angry. "Nate went to college. He didn't know I changed my mind."

Why didn't you tell him? The question was punctuated with sharp, heated hand movements.

Omitting the part about his grandparents suggesting to Nate that she'd miscarried—because some truths could wait forever—Izzy tried to explain the feelings that had led her to raise Eli on her own.

"I was afraid. Afraid to be hurt. Afraid to risk being rejected by Nate or his parents. Afraid to have them reject you because of me. Eli, I love you more than anything." Spontaneously, she placed her hand on his arm. He reacted as if her touch burned. Swallowing the pain that caused, she continued, "What I didn't know then was that trying to avoid pain just prolongs it. I made mistakes. Nate... your father—"

Don't call him that.

Izzy lowered her head, took a breath, then continued. "He's a good man, Eli. I don't think I realized how good until I saw how much he wants to get to know you. How very much he wants to love you."

Tears filled her son's eyes. "I don't want to get to know him!" He used ASL and his voice this time. "And I want you to leave."

"Eli, we're human. Human beings blow it. Sometimes we blow it really badly."

He sat up, this time using his hands and shouting.

"That's your excuse?" Jumping from the bed, he stalked the room like a caged animal. "Great. So the next time I lie or do something I know is messed up, I can just say, 'Sorry, Mom, I'm human, so get off my case'?"

There had been so many parenting moments when she'd felt in over her head, but never like this. As hard as it was to let her child hurt, she could accept that pain was part of growing up. But this much pain?

"I love you. And when you're ready to forgive us, you're going to find out that you have *two* parents who love you and want the very best for you."

"I'm never going to be ready to forgive you for this. Go away!"

She stood her ground, matching his intensity. "I love you."

"Leave me alone, Mom."

I love you. She signed it, hard.

"Leave!"

The bedroom door swung open. Izzy hadn't heard footsteps and was caught by surprise when Nate appeared, filling the room with his tall, imposing, unapologetic presence. He looked like…a father. "Don't talk to your mother that way. If you want to blame someone, blame me, but she's earned your respect."

"You're telling me what to do? Seriously?" He turned to his mother and signed, *What a jerk.*

Eli, stop, Izzy signed back. For the first time in her life, she saw her son sneer.

Nate got right in the boy's face. "Your fight is with me. I left—she didn't."

"Fine. You both suck."

"Eli!" Izzy jumped between them. "Apologize."

Nate grabbed her arm, applying a gentle pressure while he addressed Eli. "No one's telling you you're not entitled to be angry. But your mother doesn't deserve to bear the brunt of it. No one has ever done more for you. She's worth ten of me." He paused briefly. "She's worth ten of anyone else."

Eli looked from Nate to his mother, then turned away, his expression still turbulent.

Izzy ached for her son. She ached for all three of them, but when she looked at Nate, she felt less alone than ever before.

Seated at the desk in his room at the inn, Nate attempted to concentrate on the plans Jax Stewart had asked him to draft for a green remodel of a sizable portion of the downtown area. Ordinarily, the project would easily claim his focus, but it had been two days since he'd left Izzy's after the confrontation with Eli, and he'd been jumpy as a cat ever since.

Izzy had encouraged him to give Eli some time. That might have been easier if he could have seen her in the interim, but she'd been sticking as close as possible to their son.

Closing the lid on his laptop with far too much force, Nate leaned back in the chair, tilting it on two legs. He was jealous.

Izzy had texted him an encouraging note this morning, urging him to be patient and have faith. Be patient? Picking up a pencil, he chucked it across the room. *There's your patience.*

Eli would be a man before they blinked. He wanted time with his son, damn it. He wanted…

Everything. Eli. Izzy. He wanted to know it wasn't too late. And he wanted to know it right now.

Picking up his cell phone, he tapped her number, waited one ring, hung up, tossed the phone onto his desk and dug his fingers into his hair. *Give it time…trust…*

Pushing his chair back, he rose, grabbed his room card

and headed for the door. Kissing Izzy—*that* was what he needed to do, because when he kissed her, then she felt as urgent as he did.

Flinging open the door, he headed down the hallway, arriving at the carpeted stairway in several giant strides and flying down the first flight until he reached the landing and stopped dead.

"Hi." The word was accompanied by a tip of four fingers moving from his son's forehead to form an arc in the air. In his other hand, Eli held a baseball and bat. "Are you heading out?" he asked.

"No." Nate's throat felt raw. His heart pumped like it had the first time he saw the ocean. "I mean, yeah, but… You want to come up? Or head outside? Whatever you want." *Calm down.*

Eli, looking about as comfortable as a colt in jeans, bounced the bat against his sneakers. "I play baseball."

Nate nodded. "Your mom says you're good."

"I want to pitch, but I throw too many balls. She said you pitched for the Huskies."

"I was a better football player, but, yeah, I managed to pitch the ball over home base a few times…" Emotion welled in Nate's chest. His son played on one of the same high school teams he'd played for. "I could give you a few pointers…if you want." *Don't say no.* When had he ever been this afraid of being rejected?

Eli shifted the baseball to his other hand and fingered it nervously. "If you've got time."

"Yeah." A smile began to grow in Nate's chest. "I've got all the time in the world."

Heaven on earth. That was what teaching his son to pitch a fastball felt like—heaven right here in Thunder Ridge. Now they were eating ice-cream cones—and he finally knew his son's favorite flavor: mint cookie dough—on a bench overlooking Long River.

I'm a dad, damn it. He had to keep from grinning. Eli was still a hard sell; they weren't as easy with each other as they'd been before the big reveal, but once Nate's pitching suggestions had helped put the ball into the strike zone, Eli had started to warm up again. Speaking of the big reveal...

"Hey, how did you know I'm your—" He stumbled.

"Father?" Eli supplied. The boy rubbed his eyes before he answered, a gesture that reminded Nate of himself. "I knew something was going on. My mom never invites guys over. And then the day we were on the river, you took off your shirt."

Nate looked at him quizzically.

"You have the Island of Manhattan. Like me."

"The what?"

Eli smiled. "It's what my mom calls my birthmark. Here." He pointed to his rib cage. "It's shaped like Manhattan."

Nate's jaw lowered. "We have the same birthmark?"

Eli took a couple of licks of his cone. "Pretty close. I never used to like it."

"Me, either," Nate related, feeling dazed. *We have the same birthmark.* It was one more awe-inspiring tie.

"Yours is paler. I don't mind mine so much anymore." He shrugged. "It's part of me."

"Yeah." Part of Eli. Part of Nate. "I don't mind mine, either." He went ahead and grinned. *My boy and I are a lot alike.* "I don't mind it one bit."

Chapter Seventeen

"'Happy Forty-Fifth Birthday, Pickle Jar,'" Derek read the sign Izzy had hung across the wall above a bank of booths in the deli. "Shouldn't that be 'Happy Anniversary'?"

From her vantage point behind the counter, where platters of smoked fish, trays of vegetables and mini brisket sandwiches tempted the guests, Izzy cocked her head at the sign. "Now that you mention it, probably. But Sam and Henry never had kids. The Pickle Jar really is their baby, so birthday seems apropos."

"I suppose." Derek finished a tea-sized corned beef on rye in two bites. "So, how's it going, Izz?"

Looking around at a deli filled with friends and neighbors, with her coworkers passing trays of knishes, bite-size kugels and other delights, Izzy answered honestly, "Good. I mean, we're still walking the line between red and black, but I've great promo ideas. I even think we can build an online presence. I'm thinking about starting a pickle blog."

"Wow. Subscribe me. But I wasn't talking about the

restaurant." He nodded to a booth where Nate and Eli sat on one side, talking to Sam and Henry, who were on the other. "I meant *that.*"

She followed his gaze. "Oh." As usual when she talked to Derek about Eli lately, equal measures of pleasure and guilt washed through her. "Oh, you know. It's, uh, it's… nice."

"Nice." Derek scoffed. "You are so full of it. I see them biking all over town. It must be a lot better than nice."

"Well…" She shook her head. "Oh, Derek, I hope you know Eli loves you. I mean *loves* you. You're family, and no one is ever going to take your place—"

"Izz," he stopped her. "You've told me that forty-three times. Since this morning." Wiping his hands on a napkin, he put his palms companionably on her shoulders. "Eli and I hung out yesterday at the batting cage in Doc Howard Park."

"You did?"

"Yes. Got a soda afterward. We're good. He seems happy."

Izzy felt her stomach muscles relax. She nodded. "He is."

"All right, then." Derek let go of her to snag a passing knish. "What about you and Thayer?"

Oops, there went her stomach muscles again. "Nate and I?" Fiddling with the veggie tray, she shook her head. "We're focusing on Eli. On co-parenting. We're not really… you know, because there's so much work to be done to get everyone on the right track, and I've been so busy with the deli and putting together this party, and—"

"Is she talking about Nate again?" Holliday strolled up, parking herself on a counter stool in front of the lox on baby bagels. "*So* yummy," she purred, raising the hors d'oeuvre. "Nate *and* the food," she clarified. "You are talking about him, aren't you? It sounds like it. You hyper-babble when his name comes up."

"That's not true. I have nothing to hyper-babble about. There's nothing going on."

Derek smirked. Holliday laughed outright. "When was the last time you kissed him?"

"Last night around midnight," Derek supplied the requested information. "They were at the gazebo. Mrs. Kaminsky saw them."

"Really?" Holliday looked delighted.

"Mrs. Kaminsky saw us?" Izzy yelped, looking around to make sure nobody heard. "What was that old woman doing out at midnight?" she hissed.

"Walking Little Pete. He ate a triple-scoop waffle cone someone dropped on the sidewalk. That's a lot of dairy for a Chihuahua. Apparently, he had the trots all night."

"Aw," Holliday sympathized. "I love Little Pete."

"Yeah, he's a good dog."

"Will you two stop it," Izzy snapped, concerned about the gossip that must be swirling around town. "If Mrs. Kaminsky saw us and told you, then she probably told other people, too, right? Half the town must know by now."

"Half the town already knows you and Nate are sneaking around," Holliday said around another bite of mini bagel. They think it's cute."

"What?"

"That's not true," Derek scoffed.

"Thank goodness." Izzy sighed.

"The *whole* town knows. And they do think it's cute. Matter of fact, Mark Gooding, the sheriff over in Bristol—remember the one I tried to fix you up with?—he phoned this afternoon. Said to tell you good luck."

Izzy gasped. "No! You've got to be kidding."

"I am kidding," Derek assured her. "About Mark. But what's the big deal, Izz?"

"Yes. You're parents," Holliday pointed out. "Everyone will be thrilled for you. No one is judging."

"I'm sure some of them are, but I'm not worried about that," Izzy insisted. "I don't want Eli to get any ideas. To get his hopes up. You saw *The Parent Trap*," she said to Holly. "You know."

"The parents in that movie wind up together. It has a happy ending."

"But it's a movie!" She spread her hands. "Nate and I dating puts Eli in a very vulnerable position."

"So what are you doing? Waiting to see if it sticks before you tell anyone?" Holliday asked.

Izzy nodded. "Seems like a good plan."

"Well, I don't get it." Holly shook her head. Then she leaned close to Izzy and asked, her voice low, "Do you love him?"

Izzy figured she might as well answer that honestly, since everyone seemed to know her business anyway. She even opened her mouth to do it, but the musical tap of silverware on a water glass interrupted her.

"May I have your attention?" Henry Bernstein stood in front of the booth where he'd been talking to Sam and Nate and Eli. "I have a few things I'd like to say."

Izzy, Holliday and Derek cut their conversation short and faced their host.

"Forty-five years is a good long life for a restaurant," Henry continued. "Longer than some marriages, and definitely longer than I kept my hair." Laughter bubbled around the restaurant. "We couldn't have arrived at this place without help. Especially from wonderful, loyal employees, many of whom I've come to think of as family." He motioned for Sam to join him. Wiry and still spry, Sam slid out of the booth to stand beside his brother. "Sammy and I, we're about as lucky as two average Joes can get. We've had great lives. My brother pointed out recently that we're not getting any younger, and although I certainly think *I* am—"

There was more laughter and some applause. Derek whistled through his teeth and called out, "You're a pup!"

Izzy wanted to laugh along, but a strong foreboding crept into her.

Henry nodded impishly. "Yes, well, my brother also pointed out, quite wisely, that there really is a life beyond the walls of The Pickle Jar."

"That's only a rumor!" called Oliver.

Leon added, "Yeah, that's never been proven, boss."

Henry patted the air. "Okay, okay. What has been proven is that newer restaurants, owned by younger people, are doing better in this town than we are."

Izzy wanted to shout, *Stop!* She wanted this conversation, wherever it was heading, to happen in the office, not out here.

"What you don't know," Henry continued, "is that our building was purchased recently. The whole block was purchased, in fact, by someone young and energetic. Someone with a very good vision for change and for growth. Sammy and I want to step aside to make room for that change, that youthful spark, because, believe it or not, we were that spark once. We know it can be a powerful thing."

This can't be happening. It can't be. Not now. Izzy felt an urge to scream that felt very much like hysteria. *We need this restaurant. It's our home. We're family—*

"Nate, stand up with us," Henry requested. Appearing confident and so handsome that at any other time it would have taken Izzy's breath away, Nate rose from the booth, standing tall and square shouldered next to the Bernstein brothers. His gaze met Izzy's.

"This is an exciting time for our town," Henry said. He reached up to clamp a hand on Nate's shoulder. "And this is one of the people who is going to make it exciting. Nate

Thayer left here an eighteen-year-old boy with a dream to become an architect."

Was it Izzy's imagination or was Nate nervous beneath the calm and composed air?

"He has returned," Henry continued, "an architect of some renown, and it is his desire to contribute to the rebirth of Thunder Ridge. The town we all love should be a relevant player on the Oregon landscape."

Izzy stared, agape with an awful fascination, the way one would watch cars on an inevitable collision course.

"Nate will be working for the new owner of the building we are standing in. Together, they have plans to beautify the entire block. To bring in more business, which will mean more jobs and bigger paychecks. I'll let him say a few words about his plans. Plus, we have another surprise for you. I think I'll let him spill the beans on that one, too. Nate, it's your turn."

"Thanks, Henry."

Izzy couldn't hear. Literally could not hear. She plastered a smile on her face so no one would see the storm inside her. With all the attention at the front of the room, she backed up a few steps and then a few steps more until she was at the entrance to the kitchen. Grabbing an empty tray from the work counter, she turned and fled.

The building was sold. Nate was working with the new owner to "improve" the entire block, and Henry and Sam wanted to retire.

Tears filled her eyes. Anger, frustration, grief jumbled together.

How could Nate? How could he have known all this was coming and not said a word to her? No warning at all?

If the building was remodeled, the new owner would raise the rent—

Forget the rent, dummy. Henry and Sam are retiring. New businesses...new opportunities. The Pickle Jar had seen its heyday. And all her efforts to bring that heyday back had been for naught. They were going to close and make way for something shiny and new and "relevant."

Rushing to the back door, Izzy slipped into the alley and took deep gulps of the night air.

How could this be happening? Why hadn't she paid attention to the signs? There were always signs. Like Sam speaking so admiringly of the retirement home. And Henry talking about not visiting Hawaii since his honeymoon and wondering how it had changed. But Nate—

There hadn't been any signs to tell her that Nate was going to aid and abet in pulling the rug out from under her. Without a word. Without a warning.

Izzy pressed a hand to her forehead, which was starting to pound already. Every cell in her body seemed to be captured by fear and foreboding. It felt intolerable, and she started to walk. Fast and then faster.

She walked to her house, grabbed Latke, who was delighted to see her, got on her bike and pedaled in the dark, her dog trotting somewhat warily alongside. On the way, her phone buzzed. Pulling way off to the side of the road, she checked her messages while Latke sniffed the weeds. She had a text from Eli, one from Derek and another from Nate.

Eli's read: Mom, why rn't u here? This is so gr8!

Her son thought losing the deli was great? Maybe that was how everyone would feel about a modern, convenient, stupid new district that would look like a million other modern, convenient, stupid new shopping districts.

She looked at Derek's message: R U OK? TEXT OR I'LL PUT OUT AN APB.

And from Nate: Wanted to surprise you. I screwed up. Call me. Now.

Ignoring Nate, Izzy responded to Eli: Needed air and

breakfast 4 2morrow. U know me, always thinking food.
BBL8R.

Then she reassured Derek: Am FINE. No APB. Thx, tho.

She slipped the phone into her pants pocket and resumed her ride.

Her body seemed to take over from her mind. She didn't
so much *decide* where to go as she simply wound up there.

In the dark, the trailer she'd shared with Felicia looked
more ominous than it did during the day, when it was
mostly a pathetic, decrepit pile of junk. At night it seemed
haunted, and the ghosts were all Izzy's.

Latke hung back, pulling on the leash as Izzy walked
toward the broken front door. Giving in, she unclipped
the leash to let Latke wander outside while she opened the
rusted door and went in.

With the full moon as her only light source out here, she
had to sense more than see the condition of the old place,
but she wasn't interested in the aesthetics.

Tonight, she felt as though she were eight years old
again, sitting on that lopsided sofa by the window, pretending that being alone didn't frighten her.

The only time she ever stepped foot inside this miserable place nowadays was when she needed to remind herself that she was no longer terrified, no longer desperate,
no longer alone. Anytime she felt frightened or defeated
as an adult, she promised herself she would never, ever
feel as powerless as she'd felt as a child.

Except that now she did. It seemed that everything she'd
worked so ferociously to build was falling apart.

Shaking, she wandered to the sofa, but memory hit so
fast and so furiously that she stopped dead in her tracks.

There she was, at age eight, sitting on the couch, hope-
ful and frightened in the hand-me-down dress with a
torn ruffle on the skirt that she thought was so fancy. Her
mother showed up after the sky had already gone dark.

She had remembered it was Izzy's birthday and had come home, bringing a stuffed bunny for her daughter and a new boyfriend for herself. They threw Izzy a quick party by sticking a match in a Ding Dong and then put her to bed.

Her memories fast-forwarded to age twelve. On that birthday, she baked herself a pan of brownies and lit her own candles. Her mother didn't come home at all that night or the week after. Izzy had a contest going in her head, trying to see if she could outlast her mother's negligence by refusing to try to find Felicia or reminding her she'd missed her daughter's birthday. That was when Izzy promised herself she would never again beg for someone's love.

"And I didn't," she murmured, her legs so weak she felt as if she might crumple in a heap right there. She hadn't begged for Henry's and Sam's love or for her friends'; she didn't beg her coworkers to like her, and she certainly had never, ever begged for Nate's love.

The fact that she hadn't told him *I love you* in actual words had been a source of pride and comfort when she was seventeen.

Tears that were decades old got stuck in her throat, feeling like a lump of tar. She was afraid to cry, afraid she would be unable to stop, but it ceased to be her choice. Doubled over, as if protecting the little girl who'd refused to cry all those years ago, she sobbed, the sound echoing through the shell of a house that had heard much noise but little genuine emotion.

Responding to her mommy's crying, Latke braved the rusty steps and entered the trailer. Whining, she shoved her broad nose against Izzy's leg. Kneeling next to Latke, Izzy gathered her dog in a fierce hug as she wept in pain. She cried in recognition, too, because the truth was that she wasn't alone anymore. Henry, Sam, Eli and Derek and Holliday—they never missed her birthday, even when she told them not to bother.

She had learned to give her love to people who were capable of loving her back, and she'd come to trust that they weren't going to leave. Could she really choose to doubt all that now just because two wonderful men in their seventies had decided it was time to retire?

And what about Nate? She loved the way he looked at Eli when Eli wasn't looking. She loved the way he looked at her. When Nate grinned, she felt as light as down, and when he kissed her, the very last cracks in her heart knit together until she felt seamless, whole.

She'd thought refusing to be broken made her a winner. Maybe the willingness to be broken, knowing she would be put back together again, even stronger—maybe that was the real victory.

Trust beyond Izzy's understanding settled around her like a comforter, filling her with resolve. As the tears dried, she raised her head. Through the dark, she peered at the lifeless trailer, and the truth settled on her. *Izzy Lambert doesn't live here anymore.*

Pulling out her phone, she sent a text, then pocketed the cell again without waiting for a reply. Wiping her face, she rose and walked to the door, her loyal dog by her side. Heading out, they made their way down the steps and across the weeds to the spot where Izzy left her bike. Only then did she turn for one look at the trailer. The last look. She wouldn't need to come here again.

By the time she reached her house, Nate was there, pacing the porch. He bounded down the steps to meet her.

"Where's Eli?" she asked.

"Still at the party." He grabbed her arms. "I'm sorry. I wanted to surprise you. It was stupid. I should have realized that with all the secrets in our history—"

Izzy put her fingers on Nate's lips. "I don't want to talk about the past. Thank you for meeting me." She gazed into his worried features, so perfect, so intense. Taking his hand, she led him to the porch, but neither of them wanted to sit.

"I've already been here once," he said, "and to the grocery because of that cock-and-bull story you told Eli about needing breakfast foods, and to your favorite spot on the river. If you hadn't texted me—"

"I know. I'm sorry." She wasted no time with explanations about why she'd left the party. She didn't want to waste any more time at all. "I love you." Sounding breathless, she tried again. "I love you, and I loved you fifteen years ago, and maybe it wouldn't have mattered if I'd told you then, but I should have, just because it was the truth." The words emerged like a pent-up sigh, ready to be released at last. "We have a son, and I think we should finish raising him together— No. No, that's not right. It's not that I think we *should,* it's that I *want* to. I want to finish raising him as a team. I want us to be together." Her heart beat a mile a minute. Honesty felt dangerous and terrifying and absolutely right. "If you want us to be together, too, then great. And if you don't…" She was about to assure him they would work out the details of parenting from a distance, then shook her head. "You have to want us to be together, because this is right. This is whole. This is that thing you were talking about. It's what Henry means when he says *bashert.* You're my meant-to-be, Nate Thayer, and, darn it, I know it, and you should know it, too, and if you don't, well, then—"

Nate's kiss absorbed everything else she was going to say. A delightful dizziness replaced thoughts.

When they stopped kissing, she lowered her forehead to his shirt and breathed him in. "I can move to Chicago so you can be closer to Eli," she murmured. "I don't want you two to be apart again."

Nate held her face with one hand and kissed her forehead. "You can't come to Chicago." His response mirrored the look in his eyes—sweet and amused and loving. "You have obligations here."

"Only for a little while longer, apparently." She frowned. "Or would you rather that I not come to Chicago?"

He kissed her again, swift and hard this time, then said, "Hey, that bossy confidence thing is really sexy. Don't louse it up now."

Izzy pushed away from him. "All right, then tell me what you mean."

"That's better." He grinned. "I mean, you left the party too soon. And we were clumsy about the way we made the announcement. You, Isabelle Lambert—someday hopefully—Thayer, are the new co-owner of The Pickle Jar. Fifty-one percent interest with Henry and Sam as your mostly silent partners. The deli will have to close temporarily during the remodel, which you will work on with me, so that I understand your vision for the restaurant. Then The Pickle Jar will reopen as part of a green remodel of the downtown blocks. Jax inherited a couple buildings and bought quite a few others, but he isn't going to rent-gouge or squeeze people out. He's looking at a few-years-long project intended to make Thunder Ridge a more relevant tourist destination during ski season and in the summer. Too many people stay outside of town and come to the Ridge just to ski. Jax wants to keep them and their wallets right here. I've been looking for a project exactly like this. There'll be plenty more in Oregon, too."

Nate looked immensely pleased with himself. "And," he said, "your employees can temporarily go on unemployment or accept a stipend while the deli is closed. Jax found an anonymous donor to help out. Same for the other businesses that will be affected." He laughed. "You look stunned."

Izzy nodded. "Did you say Isabelle Lambert—someday hopefully—Thayer?"

It took Nate a second or two. "With everything I just told you, that's what you want to know?"

She nodded.

A slow smile spread across his face. "Good." He leaned close so close that no one, not even the crickets chirping all around them, could have heard him. "I want to stay in Thunder Ridge, with you and Eli. I feel better standing still right here than I ever felt chasing success anyplace else." Reaching into his pocket, he pulled out a dark blue velvet box, opened the lid and dropped to one knee before her. "Izzy Lambert, will you marry me? So that the rest of our lives can begin right now?"

Izzy couldn't believe what she was hearing. Or seeing. Nestled inside the jewelry box, a platinum ring with three diamonds sparkled beneath the porch lights. A family of multifaceted gems nestled together.

This was the life she hadn't dared dream about. "You're moving awfully quickly," she demurred, not meaning a word of it. "We've hardly dated, and you want to get married. What kind of example is that to set for our son?" Happy tears slipped down her cheeks.

Nate rose and gently thumbed the tears away. "I asked Eli for his blessing first. He gave it. We've waited fifteen years, Isabel. The way I felt with you—it was always there in the back of my mind, no matter what I was doing or whom I was with. I've been trying to recapture that feeling for half my life."

"What feeling would that be?"

Nate kissed her again, long and slow and thoroughly. "That one," he murmured when they parted. "The one that tells me there's nothing I need or want that I don't already have. The feeling that heaven is right here in my arms. That's the feeling I want every day for the rest of my life. Do you want it, too?"

"I do," Izzy agreed, feeling as if her heart might explode

with joy when he took her hand and placed his ring on her finger. The ring was exquisite, but nothing could match the beauty of Nate's expression when she looked into his eyes and vowed, "For better, for worse, for always. I definitely, definitely do."

Epilogue

Eli stood next to his dad, beneath the gazebo in Doc Howard Park. *You look nervous*, he signed to Nate. *You should breathe or something.*

Not nervous, Nate signed back. *Excited.* He tugged his tie as if it was way too tight, shrugged and signed again, *A little nervous, maybe.*

Eli grinned. Smiling came easily around his dad. *His dad.* Okay, it was still totally surreal to think those words, much less say them.

In the four months since Nate had come back to town, there had been a lot of changes in Thunder Ridge. Several of the stores, including The Pickle Jar, were closed for renovations. With the deli dark, his mom had had a lot of time on her hands, which had turned out to be a giant pain. She fed everyone like every five minutes and registered Uncle Derek on an internet dating site until he told her to back off. Finally, Nate had suggested she stop butting into everyone's business and start doing something useful, like plan their wedding.

His mom's face had gone through probably a thousand different expressions before she'd burst into tears. It had taken his dad a couple of minutes to figure out that all the blubbering meant "yes."

So, they were going to be a family—officially—in three… two…one…

Right now.

As LeeAnne Alves, the music teacher at the elementary school, played the wedding march on her flute, his mom walked toward the gazebo. Henry held one of her arms, and Sam held the other.

My grandpas. The thought came unbidden, surprising Eli and making him feel kinda weird. Sort of…sentimental about his whole life.

His grandmother—his dad's mom—was here, too. Eli didn't know her too well yet, and she seemed really awkward sometimes, but when he took a peek at her now, she was watching them and smiling as if she was really happy.

Everyone he and his mom knew was sitting in the folding chairs set up on the grass. Uncle Derek was in the front row. He made eye contact with Eli and signed, *Your mom and Nate look like they need oxygen.*

Eli nodded. *Scared of crowds.*

Wimps. Your mom looks pretty.

Eli looked at his mother. Wow. Yeah, she did.

Her dress was long with skinny straps on the shoulders, and the color was almost exactly the shade of pink in the sunset. Her gaze remained glued to his father, who walked down the gazebo steps to meet her. For just a second as they grasped each other's hands, a glow surrounded them, and they seemed to forget that anyone else was there, even Eli.

Suddenly, he felt nearly grown up and really, really

young again, all at once. His heart pinched in a not totally good way. But then his parents started toward the steps, and when his mother reached them, he saw tears sparkling in her eyes.

Letting go of Nate's hand, she passed her bouquet to Holliday and signed to Eli, *I love you so much. Ready, First Mate?*

Was he ready?

As Eli glanced at his dad, he remembered something. A couple of weeks ago, they'd been in this park, tossing a baseball around, and Eli had missed a catch. When he'd run to the bench where the ball had rolled, he had seen a guy with a real little baby in a stroller. That guy had been watching his baby just the way Nate was watching him and his mom now. Like he was sort of amazed by them and also determined to watch over them every day, forever.

Man, being on the receiving end of that kind of attention was going to get annoying.

This time Eli's smile began from deep inside, replacing the pinched feeling around his heart.

Meeting his mom's eyes, he signed back, *Ready, Skipper. Totally ready.*

He took her right arm and Nate took her left as they faced the minister—and their future—together.

* * * * *

Will Sheriff Neel find his perfect match?
Look for his story,
the next installment in
Wendy Warren's new miniseries
THE MEN OF THUNDER RIDGE
Coming soon to Harlequin Special Edition!

Officer Wyn Bailey has found herself wanting more from her boss—and older brother's best friend— for a while now. Will sexy police chief Cade Emmett let his guard down long enough to embrace the love he secretly craves?

Read on for a sneak peek at the newest book in New York Times *bestselling author RaeAnne Thayne's* HAVEN POINT *series,* *RIVERBEND ROAD,* *available July 2016 from HQN Books.*

CHAPTER ONE

"THIS WAS YOUR dire emergency? Seriously?"

Officer Wynona Bailey leaned against her Haven Point Police Department squad car, not sure whether to laugh or pull out her hair. "That frantic phone call made it sound like you were at death's door!" she exclaimed to her great-aunt Jenny. "You mean to tell me I drove here with full lights and sirens, afraid I would stumble over you bleeding on the ground, only to find you in a standoff with a baby moose?"

The gangly-looking creature had planted himself in the middle of the driveway while he browsed from the shrubbery that bordered it. He paused in his chewing to watch the two of them out of long-lashed dark eyes.

He was actually really cute, with big ears and a curious face. She thought about pulling out her phone to take a picture that her sister could hang on the local wildlife bulletin board in her classroom but decided Jenny probably wouldn't appreciate it.

"It's not the calf I'm worried about," her great-aunt said. "It's his mama over there."

She followed her aunt's gaze and saw a female moose on the other side of the willow shrubs, watching them with much more caution than her baby was showing.

While the creature might look docile on the outside, Wyn knew from experience a thousand-pound cow could move at thirty-five miles an hour and wouldn't hesitate to take on anything she perceived as a threat to her offspring.

"I need to get into my garage, that's all," Jenny practically wailed. "If Baby Bullwinkle there would just move two feet onto the lawn, I could squeeze around him, but he won't budge for anything."

She had to ask the logical question. "Did you try honking your horn?"

Aunt Jenny glared at her, looking as fierce and stern as she used to when Wynona was late turning in an assignment in her aunt's high school history class.

"Of course I tried honking my horn! And hollering at the stupid thing and even driving right up to him, as close as I could get, which only made the mama come over to investigate. I had to back up again."

Wyn's blood ran cold, imagining the scene. That big cow could easily charge the sporty little convertible her diminutive great-aunt had bought herself on her seventy-fifth birthday.

What would make them move along? Wynona sighed, not quite sure what trick might disperse a couple of stubborn moose. Sure, she was trained in Krav Maga martial arts, but somehow none of those lessons seemed to apply in this situation.

The pair hadn't budged when she pulled up with her lights and sirens blaring in answer to her aunt's desperate phone call. Even if she could get them to move, scaring them out of Aunt Jenny's driveway would probably only migrate the problem to the neighbor's yard.

She was going to have to call in backup from the state wildlife division.

"Oh, no!" her aunt suddenly wailed. "He's starting on the honeysuckle! He's going to ruin it. Stop! Move it. Go on now." Jenny started to climb out of her car again, raising and lowering her arms like a football referee calling a touchdown.

"Aunt Jenny, get back inside your vehicle!" Wyn exclaimed.

"But the honeysuckle! Your dad planted that for me the summer before he...well, you know."

Wyn's heart gave a sharp little spasm. Yes. She *did* know. She pictured the sturdy, robust man who had once watched over his aunt, along with everybody else in town. He wouldn't have hesitated for a second here, would have known exactly how to handle the situation.

Wynnie, anytime you're up against something bigger than you, just stare `em down. More often than not, that will do the trick.

Some days, she almost felt like he was riding shotgun next to her.

"Stay in your car, Jenny," she said again. "Just wait there while I call Idaho Fish and Game to handle things. They probably need to move them to higher ground."

"I don't have time to wait for some yahoo to load up his tranq gun and hitch up his horse trailer, then drive over from Shelter Springs! Besides that honeysuckle, which is priceless to me, I have seventy-eight dollars' worth of groceries in the trunk of my car that will be ruined if I can't get into the house. That includes four pints of Ben & Jerry's Cherry Garcia that's going to be melted red goo if I don't get it in the freezer fast—and that stuff is not exactly cheap, you know."

Her great-aunt looked at her with every expectation that she would fix the problem and Wyn sighed again. Small-town police work was mostly about problem solving—and when she happened to have been born and raised in that small town, too many people treated her like their own private security force.

"I get it. But I'm calling Fish and Game."

"You've got a piece. Can't you just fire it into the air or something?"

Yeah, unfortunately, her great-aunt—like everybody else in town—watched far too many cop dramas on TV and thought that was how things were done.

"Give me two minutes to call Fish and Game, then I'll see if I can get him to move aside enough that you can pull into your driveway. Wait in your car," she ordered for the fourth time as she kept an eye on Mama Moose. "Do not, I repeat, do *not* get out again. Promise?"

Aunt Jenny slumped back into her seat, clearly disappointed that she wasn't going to have front row seats to some kind of moose-cop shoot-out. "I suppose."

To Wyn's relief, local game warden Moose Porter— who, as far as she knew, was no relation to the current troublemakers—picked up on the first ring. She explained the situation to him and gave him the address.

"You're in luck. We just got back from relocating a female brown bear and her cub away from that campground on Dry Creek Road. I've still got the trailer hitched up."

"Thanks. I owe you."

"How about that dinner we've been talking about?" he asked.

She had not been talking about dinner. Moose had been pretty relentless in asking her out for months and she always managed to deflect. It wasn't that she didn't like the guy. He was nice and funny and good-looking in a burly, outdoorsy, flannel-shirt-and-gun-rack sort of way, but she didn't feel so much as an ember around him. Not like, well, someone else she preferred not to think about.

Maybe she would stop thinking about that *someone else* if she ever bothered to go on a date. "Sure," she said on impulse. "I'm pretty busy until after Lake Haven Days, but let's plan something in a couple of weeks. Meantime, how soon can you be here?"

"Great! I'll definitely call you. And I've got an ETA of about seven minutes now."

The obvious delight left her squirming and wishing she had deflected his invitation again.

Fish or cut line, her father would have said.

"Make it five, if you can. My great-aunt's favorite honeysuckle bush is in peril here."

"On it."

She ended the phone call just as Jenny groaned, "Oh. Not the butterfly bush, too! Shoo. Go on, move!"

While she was on the phone, the cow had moved around the shrubs nearer her calf and was nibbling on the large showy blossoms on the other side of the driveway.

Wyn thought about waiting for the game warden to handle the situation, but Jenny was counting on her. She couldn't let a couple of moose get the better of her. Wondering idly if a Kevlar vest would protect her in the event she was charged, she climbed out of her patrol vehicle and edged around to the front bumper. "Come on. Move along. That's it."

She opted to move toward the calf, figuring the cow would follow her baby. Mindful to keep the vehicle between her and the bigger animal, she waved her arms like she was directing traffic in a big-city intersection. "Go. Get out of here."

Something in her firm tone or maybe her rapid-fire movements finally must have convinced the calf she wasn't messing around this time. He paused for just a second, then lurched through a break in the shrubs to the other side, leaving just enough room for Great-Aunt Jenny to squeeze past and head for her garage to unload her groceries.

"Thank you, Wynnie. You're the best," her aunt called. "Come by one of these Sundays for dinner. I'll make my fried chicken and biscuits and my Better-Than-Sex cake."

Her mouth watered and her stomach rumbled, reminding her quite forcefully that she hadn't eaten anything since her shift started that morning.

Her great-aunt's Sunday dinners were pure decadence. Wyn could almost feel her arteries clog in anticipation.

"I'll check my schedule."

"Thanks again."

Jenny drove her flashy little convertible into the garage and quickly closed the door behind her.

Of all things, the sudden action of the door seemed to startle the big cow moose where all other efforts—including a honking horn and Wyn's yelling and arm-peddling—had failed. The moose shied away from the activity, heading in Wyn's direction.

Crap.

Heart pounding, she managed to jump into her vehicle and yank the door closed behind her seconds before the moose charged past her toward the calf.

The two big animals picked their way across the lawn and settled in to nibble Jenny's pretty red-twig dogwoods.

Crisis managed—or at least her part in it—she turned around and drove back to the street just as a pickup pulling a trailer with the Idaho Fish and Game logo came into view over the hill.

She pushed the button to roll down her window and Moose did the same. Beside him sat a game warden she didn't know. Moose beamed at her and she squirmed, wishing she had shut him down again instead of giving him unrealistic expectations.

"It's a cow and her calf," she said, forcing her tone into a brisk, businesslike one and addressing both men in the vehicle. "They're now on the south side of the house."

"Thanks for running recon for us," Moose said.

"Yeah. Pretty sure we managed to save the Ben & Jerry's, so I guess my work here is done."

The warden grinned at her and she waved and pulled onto the road, leaving her window down for the sweet-smelling June breezes to float in.

She couldn't really blame a couple of moose for wandering into town for a bit of lunch. This was a beautiful time around Lake Haven, when the wildflowers were starting to bloom and the grasses were long and lush.

She loved Haven Point with all her heart, but she found it pretty sad that the near-moose encounter was the most exciting thing that had happened to her on the job in days.

Her cell phone rang just as she turned from Clover Hill Road to Lakeside Drive. She knew by the ringtone just who was on the other end and her breathing hitched a little, like always. Those stone-cold embers she had been wondering about when it came to Moose Porter suddenly flared to thick, crackling life.

Yeah. She knew at least one reason why she didn't go out much.

She pushed the phone button on her vehicle's hands-free unit. "Hey, Chief."

"Hear you had a little excitement this afternoon and almost tangled with a couple of moose."

She heard the amusement in the voice of her boss—and friend—and tried not to picture Cade Emmett stretched out behind his desk, big and rangy and gorgeous, with that surprisingly sweet smile that broke hearts all over Lake Haven County.

"News travels."

"Your great-aunt Jenny just called to inform me you risked your life to save her Cherry Garcia and to tell me all about how you deserve a special commendation."

"If she really thought that, why didn't she at least give me a pint for my trouble?" she grumbled.

The police chief laughed, that rich, full laugh that made her fingers and toes tingle like she'd just run full tilt down Clover Hill Road with her arms outspread.

Curse the man.

"You'll have to take that up with her next time you see

her. Meantime, we just got a call about possible trespassers at that old wreck of a barn on Darwin Twitchell's horse property on Conifer Drive, just before the turnoff for Riverbend. Would you mind checking it out before you head back for the shift change?"

"Who called it in?"

"Darwin. Apparently, somebody tripped an alarm he set up after he got hit by our friendly local graffiti artist a few weeks back."

Leave it to the ornery old buzzard to set a trap for unsuspecting trespassers. Knowing Darwin and his contrariness, he probably installed infrared sweepers and body heat sensors, even though the ramshackle barn held absolutely nothing of value.

"The way my luck is going today, it's probably a relative to the two moose I just made friends with."

"It could be a skunk, for all I know. But Darwin made me swear I'd send an officer to check it out. Since the graffiti case is yours, I figured you'd want first dibs, just in case you have the chance to catch them red-handed. Literally."

"Gosh, thanks."

He chuckled again and the warmth of it seemed to ease through the car even through the hollow, tinny Bluetooth speakers.

"Keep me posted."

"Ten-four."

She turned her vehicle around and headed in the general direction of her own little stone house on Riverbend Road that used to belong to her grandparents.

The Redemption mountain range towered across the lake, huge and imposing. The snow that would linger in the moraines and ridges above the timberline for at least another month gleamed in the afternoon sunlight and the lake was that pure, vivid turquoise usually seen only in shallow Caribbean waters.

Her job as one of six full-time officers in the Haven Point Police Department might not always be overflowing with excitement, but she couldn't deny that her workplace surroundings were pretty gorgeous.

She spotted the first tendrils of black smoke above the treetops as she turned onto the rutted lane that wound its way through pale aspen trunks and thick pines and spruce.

Probably just a nearby farmer burning some weeds along a ditch line, she told herself, or trying to get rid of the bushy-topped invasive phragmites reeds that could encroach into any marshy areas and choke out all the native species. But something about the black curl of smoke hinted at a situation beyond a controlled burn.

Her stomach fluttered with nerves. She hated fire calls even more than the dreaded DD—domestic disturbance. At least in a domestic situation, there was some chance she could defuse the conflict. Fire was avaricious and relentless, smoke and flame and terror. She had learned that lesson on one of her first calls as a green-as-grass rookie police officer in Boise, when she was the first one on scene to a deadly house fire on a cold January morning that had killed three children in their sleep.

Wyn rounded the last bend in the road and saw, just as feared, the smoke wasn't coming from a ditch line or a controlled burn of a patch of invading plants. Instead, it twisted sinuously into the sky from the ramshackle barn on Darwin Twitchell's property.

She scanned the area for kids and couldn't see any. What she did see made her blood run cold—two small boys' bikes resting on their sides outside the barn.

Where there were bikes, there were usually boys to ride them.

She parked her vehicle and shoved open her door. "Hello? Anybody here?" she called.

She strained her ears but could hear nothing above the crackle of flames. Heat and flames poured off the building.

She pressed the button on the radio at her shoulder to call dispatch. "I've got a structure fire, an old barn on Darwin Twitchell's property on Conifer Drive, just before Riverbend Road. The upper part seems to be fully engulfed and there's a possibility of civilians inside, juveniles. I've got bikes here but no kids in sight. I'm still looking."

While she raced around the building, she heard the call go out to the volunteer fire department and Chief Gallegos respond that his crews were six minutes out.

"Anybody here?" she called again.

Just faintly, she thought she heard a high cry in response, but her radio crackled with static at that instant and she couldn't be sure. A second later, she heard Cade's voice.

"Bailey, this is Chief Emmett. What's the status of the kids? Over."

She hurried back to her vehicle and popped the trunk. "I can't see them," she answered tersely, digging for a couple of water bottles and an extra T-shirt she kept back there. "I'm going in."

"Negative!" Cade's urgency fairly crackled through the radio. "The first fire crew's ETA is now four minutes. Stand down."

She turned back to the fire and was almost positive the flames seemed to be crackling louder, the smoke billowing higher into the sky. She couldn't stand the thought of children being caught inside that hellish scene. She couldn't. She pushed away the memory of those tiny charred bodies.

Maybe whoever had tripped Darwin's alarms—maybe the same kids who likely set the fire—had run off into the surrounding trees. She hoped so, she really did, but her gut told her otherwise.

In four minutes, they could be burned to a crisp, just like those sweet little kids in Boise. She had to take a look.

It's what her father would have done.

You know what John Wayne would say, John Bailey's voice seemed to echo in her head. *Courage is being scared to death but saddling up anyway.*

Yeah, Dad. I know.

Her hands were sweaty with fear, but she pushed past it and focused on the situation at hand. "I'm going in," she repeated.

"Stand down, Officer Bailey. That is a direct order."

Cade ran a fairly casual—though efficient—police department and rarely pushed rank, but right now he sounded hard, dangerous.

She paused for only a second, her attention caught by sunlight glinting off one of the bikes.

"Wynona, do you copy?" Cade demanded.

She couldn't do it. She couldn't stand out here and wait for the fire department. Time was of the essence, she knew it in her bones. After five years as a police officer, she had learned to rely on her instincts and she couldn't ignore them now.

She was just going to have to disregard his order and deal with his fury later.

"I can't hear you," she lied. "Sorry. You're crackling out."

She squelched her radio to keep him out of her ears, ripped the T-shirt and doused it with her water bottle, then held it to her mouth and pushed inside.

The shift from sunlight to smoke and darkness inside the barn was disorienting. As she had seen from outside, the flames seemed to be limited for now to the upper hayloft of the barn, but the air was thick and acrid.

"Hello?" she called out. "Anybody here?"

"Yes! Help!"

"Please help!"

Two distinct, high, terrified voices came from the far end of the barn.

"Okay. Okay," she called back, her heart pounding fiercely. "Keep talking so I can follow your voice."

There was a momentary pause. "What should we say?"

"Sing a song. How about 'Jingle Bells'? Here. I'll start."

She started the words off and then stopped when she heard two young voices singing the words between sobs. She whispered a quick prayer for help and courage, then rapidly picked her way over rubble and debris as she followed the song to its source, which turned out to be two white-faced, terrified boys she knew.

Caleb and Lucas Keegan were crouched together just below a ladder up to the loft, where the flames sizzled and popped overhead.

Caleb, the older of the two, was stretched out on the ground, his leg bent at an unnatural angle.

"Hey, Caleb. Hey, Luke."

They both sobbed when they spotted her. "Officer Bailey. We didn't mean to start the fire! We didn't mean to!" Luke, the younger one, was close to hysteria, but she didn't have time to calm him.

"We can worry about that later. Right now, we need to get out of here."

"We tried, but Caleb broked his leg! He fell and he can't walk. I was trying to pull him out, but I'm not strong enough."

"I told him to go without me," the older boy, no more than ten, said through tears. "I screamed and screamed at him, but he wouldn't go."

"We're all getting out of here." She ripped the wet cloth in half and handed a section to each boy.

Yeah, she knew the whole adage—taught by the airline industry, anyway—about taking care of yourself before turning your attention to helping others, but this case was worth an exception.

"Caleb, I'm going to pick you up. It's going to hurt, especially if I bump that broken leg of yours, but I don't have time to give you first aid."

"It doesn't matter. I don't care. Do what you have to do. We have to get Luke out of here!"

Her eyes burned from the smoke and her throat felt tight and achy. If she had time to spare, she would have wept at the boy's quiet courage. "I'm sorry," she whispered. She scooped him up into a fireman's carry, finally appreciating the efficiency of the hold. He probably weighed close to eighty pounds, but adrenaline gave her strength.

Over the crackles and crashes overhead, she heard him swallow a scream as his ankle bumped against her.

"Luke, grab hold of my belt buckle, right there in the back. That's it. Do not let go, no matter what. You hear me?"

"Yes," the boy whispered.

"I can't carry you both. I wish I could. You ready?"

"I'm scared," Luke whimpered through the wet T-shirt wrapped around his mouth.

So am I, kiddo. She forced a confident smile she was far from feeling. "Stay close to me. We're tough. We can do this."

The pep talk was meant for herself, more than the boys. Flames had finally begun crawling down the side of the barn and it didn't take long for the fire to slither its way through the old hay and debris scattered through the place.

She did *not* want to run through those flames, but her dad's voice seemed to ring again in her ears.

You never know how strong you are until being strong is the only choice you've got.

Okay, okay. She got it, already.

She ran toward the door, keeping Caleb on her shoulder with one hand while she wrapped her other around Luke's neck.

They were just feet from the door when the younger boy stumbled and went down. She could hear the flames growling louder and knew the dry, rotten barn wood was going to combust any second.

With no time to spare, she half lifted him with her other arm and dragged them all through the door and into the sunshine while the fire licked and growled at their heels.

* * * * *

Don't miss RIVERBEND ROAD by New York Times
bestselling author RaeAnne Thayne,
available July 2016 wherever HQN books
and ebooks are sold.

www.Harlequin.com

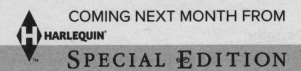

"Am I awful?"

"Awful? What in the world would make you think that?"

"Because…because…" She put her face in her hands.

At once Ryker squatted beside her, worried, touching her arm. "Marisa? What's wrong?"

"Nothing. It's just… I shouldn't be having these feelings."

"What feelings?" Suicidal thoughts? Urges to kill someone? Fear? The whole palette of emotions lay there waiting for her to choose one.

She kept her face covered. "I have dreams about you."

His entire body leaped. He had dreams about her, too, and not only when he was sleeping. "And?"

"I want you. Is that wrong? I mean…it hasn't been that long…"

Her words deprived him of breath. He could have lifted her right then and carried her to her bed. He'd have done so joyfully. But caution and maybe even some wisdom held him back.

"I want you, too," he said huskily.

She dropped her hands, her wondering eyes meeting his almost shyly. "Really? Looking like this?"

"You're beautiful looking just like that. But…"

"But?" She seized on the word, some of the wonder leaving her face.

"I don't want you to regret it. So how about we spend more time talking to each other? Give yourself some time to be sure. Hell, it probably wouldn't be safe anyway."

"My doc says it would."

She'd asked her doctor? A thousand explosions went off in his head, leaving him almost blind. He cleared his throat. "Uh…I could take you right now. I want to. So, please, don't be embarrassed. I don't think you're awful. But…please… get to know me a bit better. I want to know you better. I want you to be sure."

"I feel guilty," she admitted. "It's been driving me nuts. Am I betraying Johnny?"

"I don't believe he'd think so. But that's a question only you can answer, and you need to do that for yourself. Then there's me."

"You?" She studied him.

"I don't exactly feel right about this. After what you've already been through, I shouldn't have to explain that. I'm just like John, Marisa. Why in the world would you want to risk that again?"

She nodded slowly, looking down at where her fingertips pressed into the wooden table. "I don't know," she finally said quietly.

Don't miss
AN UNLIKELY DADDY
by New York Times *bestselling author Rachel Lee,*
available August 2016 wherever
Harlequin® *Special Edition books and ebooks are sold.*

www.Harlequin.com

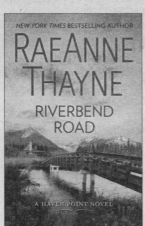

Turn your love of reading into rewards you'll love with
Harlequin My Rewards

**Join for FREE today at
www.HarlequinMyRewards.com**

Earn **FREE BOOKS** of your choice.

Experience **EXCLUSIVE OFFERS** and contests.

Enjoy **BOOK RECOMMENDATIONS**
selected just for you.

PLUS! Sign up now
and get **500** points
right away!

Earn
FREE
REWARDS
HarlequinMyRewards.com
Join
Today!

MYR16R

THE WORLD IS BETTER WITH

Romance

Harlequin has everything from contemporary, passionate and heartwarming to suspenseful and inspirational stories.

Whatever your mood, we have a romance just for you!

Connect with us to find your next great read, special offers and more.

f /HarlequinBooks

@HarlequinBooks

www.HarlequinBlog.com

www.Harlequin.com/Newsletters

HARLEQUIN®

A *Romance* FOR EVERY MOOD™

www.Harlequin.com

SERIESHALOAD2015